Penguin Books
DISPLACED P

Graeme Drury is s
looking person of
casually and gets a
friends. In fact, th

The change beg
feels that people are ignoring him. Why?
Waitresses, tram conductors—even his parents
and girl friend—are looking right through him as if
he doesn't exist.

And as he becomes indistinct to them, they and
their world become grey and faint to him. Is he going
mad? What's going on?

Graeme explores his new world, finding that it is
not easy even to survive. The physical things of the
old world slip through his fingers.

Anyone who has felt the shock of alienation from
other people and the physical world, when
everything seems not quite real, will share
Graeme's disorientation and wonder.

Lee Harding, one of Australia's best-known science
fiction writers and anthologists, was born in Colac,
Victoria, in 1937. Since 1960 his stories have
appeared regularly in British, American and
Australian publications. In 1980 *Displaced Person*
won The Australian Children's Book of the Year
Award. Lee Harding is a full-time writer based
in Melbourne. He has three grown-up children.

Displaced Person

Lee Harding

PENGUIN BOOKS

PENGUIN BOOKS

Published by the Penguin Group
27 Wrights Lane, London W8 5TZ, England
Viking Penguin Inc., 40 West 23rd Street, New York, New York 10010, USA
Penguin Books Australia Ltd, Ringwood, Victoria, Australia
Penguin Books Canada Ltd, 2801 John Street, Markham, Ontario, Canada L3R 1B4
Penguin Books (NZ) Ltd, 182–190 Wairau Road, Auckland 10, New Zealand

Penguin Books Ltd, Registered Offices: Harmondsworth, Middlesex, England

First published in Australia by Hyland House 1979
Published in the USA as *Misplaced Persons* by Harper & Row 1979
Published in Penguin Books in Australia 1981 with some minor revisions
Published in Puffin Books in Australia 1982
Reprinted 1983 (twice), 1984, 1985
Reprinted in Puffin Books in Great Britain 1986, 1987
Reprinted in Penguin Books 1988

Copyright © Lee Harding 1979, 1981
All rights reserved

Printed and bound in Great Britain by
Cox & Wyman Ltd, Reading

Except in the United States of America, this book is sold subject
to the condition that it shall not, by way of trade or otherwise, be lent,
re-sold, hired out, or otherwise circulated without the
publisher's prior consent in any form of binding or cover other than
that in which it is published and without a similar condition
including this condition being imposed on the subsequent purchaser

CIP

Harding, Lee, 1937–
Displaced person.

First published: Melbourne: Hyland House, 1979.
ISBN 0 14 031141 6.

I. Title

A823'.3

The author wishes to thank Spike Milligan for permission to quote his poem, **Rain**

Thanks also to Jo, Mike, Chris and Paula of Swinburne Technical School, who helped

For Margaret
La Belle Dame sans Merci
Without whom . . .

All that we see or seem
is but a dream within a dream.

EDGAR ALLAN POE

THE DARKNESS is closing in. I must get something down before it becomes absolute. Jamie and Marion have gone already, taking the greyworld with them. And I sit alone in a derelict house, in some godforsaken corner of the universe, talking to a tape recorder.

The cold has gripped me so fiercely that I am afraid to move. But I must do *something*. So in this place devoid of light and life and hope and any kind of peace, I gain some comfort from the sound of my own voice.

I feel a grinding glacier inside me, pressing hard against my chest. It is the weight of all my fears and I am helpless against such a pressure, but I keep talking in the vague hope that someday, somewhere, my voice will be heard. Not that I expect anyone to believe such an extraordinary tale. I have lived for a while in a place beyond human understanding, and I do not expect to survive to tell my tale. Perhaps these tapes will endure.

Where did it all begin? If only I could be *sure*. I am convinced that the origins of my present dilemma began so long ago—and so insidiously—that they escaped my attention. The closest I can get to a beginning is a summer evening, not very long ago. I think it was then that I first grew aware that something strange was happening to my world...

The compact cassette recorder I am using is one of those marvellous new Japanese innovations for weary businessmen—a portable secretary, small enough to slip inside your jacket pocket. I have two tapes—the one that came with the machine and the 'bonus' cartridge taped to the box.

I will have to talk fast if I am to put down everything I remember before the darkness claims me. Each tape has a maximum playing time of an hour and a half. Do I have three hours left? I have no way of knowing. I will press on regardless and try to keep my mind off the encroaching darkness.

There is so much I have to tell. I have never been very good at reproducing other people's conversation, but I will try to put down all our important dialogues as accurately as possible.

First, a beginning. My name is Graeme Drury and I live—or rather, I *used* to live—in Melbourne, Australia. I am seventeen years old and something terrible has happened to me. As far as I can ascertain it began late one evening when I wandered down to the local McDonald's to get myself a hamburger...

IT WAS close to nine-thirty. The place wasn't crowded. Some families clustered around their tables, enjoying a late meal after their Sunday drive. I saw some people around my own age lounging at the counter stools and wandered over to join them. There was nobody there I recognised, and that saved me from making the effort of talking. I had been feeling curiously depressed of late—a new experience for me.

There was only one girl serving. Like just about every other eating place I knew, McDonald's had cut back on staff because of the recession. She was a tall, slender blonde with a big chest and a bored expression. I guess she was maybe twenty-five or six. I figured she had been working a long day; the strain showed. Blondes are like that; fatigue really ruins them. But she kept the burgers flowing smoothly across the aisle that separated the customers from the open kitchen, passing the brightly coloured boxes into waiting hands. I have always admired anyone who can stick with repetitious work; I wouldn't last more than half a day.

I must have made six attempts before I caught her attention. I wasn't sitting apart, mind you, from the other customers, but right there in the middle, waiting my turn. But she consistently ignored me. When she finally took my order—one cheeseburger with coleslaw—I tried to relax. I had felt a lot of tension building up inside me during the past week, and I was at a loss to explain why. I had developed a nagging suspicion that fate was not being particularly kind to me. *Just a low period,* I kept telling myself. *Nothing to worry about. It will pass over. Just take it easy.* Having to shout to get my order in had not helped my jangled nerves.

I waited. And I *waited.* Three guys came in after me—truckies—and somehow managed to collect their enormous and elaborately packaged dinners and take off, while I was left waiting. I grew restless, then angry. And for the first time I understood the reason behind my tension: People were ignoring me. *Why?*

There were now only two other people seated at the counter: a young guy and his girl. They were taking their time over their burgers and chips and Coke, and talking in that dreamy, subdued way that lovers practise. That made me even more depressed. Annette should have been there with me, but for some reason I had been unable to fathom she was not. What the hell was going on?

I waited another minute. The blonde behind the counter was leaning casually over the shelf that separated her from the kitchen and was swapping small talk with the cook. I called out loudly—and, I think, very rudely—in an effort to draw her attention. Eventually she turned around and looked at me with a peculiarly blank expression, as though she had never seen me before.

'Miss,' I said, as politely and as patiently as I could manage under the circumstances, 'I am *still* waiting for my order. I gave it to you nearly a half hour ago.' And I went on to explain—very carefully, so as not to ruffle her feelings any more than I thought necessary—exactly what I had ordered, and why the blazes was it taking so long? If three truckies had come in and made off with their dinners, why had I been kept waiting?

Her expression hardly altered. 'I . . . I'm very sorry,' she apologised—and seemed genuine enough. Perhaps it had been an unusually hard day for her. Still . . .

'Ah, what was your order again, please?' She looked at me enquiringly.

I went over it again, very slowly. I was disturbed by the vague look in her eyes. Her manner reminded me of someone else, someone who wasn't with me and should have been.

The girl nodded, but I had a nagging suspicion that she had only half listened to me. She turned her head and repeated my order. I heard it loud and clear. That made me feel better. She leaned against the shelf and resumed gossiping with the guy working the hot plate.

I told myself the explanation was simple: The fool girl had simply forgotten to pass on my initial order. I am told that this sort of thing happens in the very best restaurants. But . . . hadn't this sort of thing been happening to me rather often over the past few weeks?

I considered the number of times I had been kept waiting in department stores and supermarkets with no one at all interested in serving me, delicatessens and cinemas where other people barged in before me. The incident at McDonald's suddenly brought a glaring picture into focus—and I didn't like what I saw.

People *were* ignoring me. Even Annette, and some of my closest friends. And at times my parents. Why?

I'm a rather ordinary-looking person, but I don't think of myself as being ugly or offensive. I am average height and dress casually and well. I know how to conduct myself in public. I weigh in at around 60 kilograms. I have sandy-coloured hair, blue eyes, and a fair complexion. I enjoy school and history as much as sports and mathematics. I like literature best. I'm what you might call an all-rounder. I have no bad habits that I'm aware of, and I get along well with my classmates, teachers and close friends. If I have a potential for anything in particular then I guess it just hasn't been tapped so far. I enjoy the company of girls and they seem to enjoy mine. I never come on too heavy with any one in particular, not even Annette.

Now all this was changing. And I couldn't understand *why*. Not only strangers but close friends were ignoring me—and the situation was getting progressively worse. I hadn't been sleeping well and this was affecting my schoolwork. I had even seriously considered the possibility that I just might be heading for some kind of a breakdown—but for the life of me I couldn't figure out why. Could it be possible that I was only imagining that these things were happening to me—a kind of persecution complex? But that seemed out of the question. I knew that paranoia was fashionable, but I didn't *have* any problems. I enjoyed life. I really loved learning. I got good grades and I had lots of friends. My parents were kind and understanding and encouraged me in all my endeavours. I was looking forward to the years of university that lay ahead. And now . . .

Another ten minutes passed by. McDonald's was now without a customer—except for myself. I felt surrounded by the stale smell of French fries, greasy hot plates and lukewarm coffee. I kept looking at the wall clock. It dawned upon me that I had been waiting nearly an hour for a simple cheeseburger.

I watched the seconds ticking away and felt a sinking feeling in my stomach. I vaguely heard the monotonous drone of conversation between the indolent waitress and her companion. My hunger had long since vanished.

Some people drifted in. The waitress welcomed them with a weary smile and got busy attending to their orders; she never once gave me so much as a glance. Soon the fresh aroma of cooking drifted from the hot plates and people crowded around me, reaching for the coloured cartons being handed out with what seemed to me astonishing speed.

My spirits had sunk so low that I could not even muster a stinging rebuke for the waitress. I sat there for a little while longer, trying to piece together a very strange jigsaw puzzle taking shape in my mind. Eventually I shook myself free of this line of thought and slid off the stool. Oblivious to the bright babble of late-night diners crowding around me I wandered out of the place. I was convinced that no matter how long I stayed around I would never get what I had asked for. That was part of the pattern. It was the nature of the pattern that puzzled and scared me. I'm sure the blonde didn't even notice me leaving . . .

I WALKED a few blocks before I boarded a tram. My head was in a mess. I didn't like what was happening, and I worked hard to rationalise a maddening sequence of events—without success.

Nearly everyone has experienced rotten service at a supermarket or a restaurant. But what about dry cleaners who continually lose track of your best jeans and hairdressers who can never recall how you like your hair styled?

I felt as though my life had been taken over by a nightmare that just wouldn't let go—and I was being drawn into it deeper every day.

Earlier in the day Annette had looked straight through me as though she was unaware that I was speaking to her, as if my presence with her on the sidewalk had no meaning whatsoever. It was not that my favourite girl had acted, well, cool toward me. More than that. She had seemed . . . detached. Distant. It made me shiver just to think about it, when only the night before . . .

We had had a really marvellous evening together with Drew and Helen. Drew's parents were away for the weekend so he invited us over for a small dinner party—something quiet that wouldn't upset the neighbours. We brought along some pizzas and put together a delightful punch. We played some jazz records, danced a little, talked a lot: about the future, ours and the world's. That sort of thing. It was cozy.

The following afternoon she passed me in the street without noticing me. I had to reach out and grab her arm and call out 'Hey!' before she even turned around. 'Wait a minute,' I said—then stopped. She looked at me strangely, in the way I have already described, and tugged gently away from me. She hardly seemed the same person.

'Annette,' I said, 'what's the matter? Something bothering you? Anything I've said? I thought—'

She made a garbled excuse about her mother being sick and having to hurry home. She apologised and I let her go. I was left standing, high and dry and feeling like a fool on the sidewalk. She had turned around and walked off without so much as a kiss or a good-bye.

The uphill rumbling of the tram jolted me back to the present. I looked around me at the rows of unsmiling faces. Typical. But . . . was I really going crazy? It seemed a possibility, but I knew if I ever convinced myself sufficiently of that, I would have enough presence of mind to go straight to Dr Birch. I was too young to start losing my marbles.

But what if the fault lay not with the outside world, as I had supposed, but somewhere deep inside *myself*?

The thought scared me. I got off the tram two stops from Alma Road and walked the rest of the way. I had a fear to work out of my system; it was new to me and the only thing that helped was walking. I couldn't have sat still for a moment longer; the anonymous, vacant stares of my fellow passengers had also unsettled me. Over the years I had grown accustomed to this sort of late-night transportation, but tonight had been different. Usually someone stares long enough to watch you step off. But no one had. The effect was sinister.

My parents were waiting up in the living room when I arrived home. They were watching an old black-and-white movie on television. Neither of them looked up when I walked in, even though I made a noisy ceremony out of closing the front door. I doubt if they even heard me return. They had certainly not noticed my departure.

Earlier, Mother had apologised about having no dinner for me. She said she had not been expecting me home, that I was 'going out.' I had asked her what had put such an idea in her head. 'That was *last* night,' I explained. 'Saturday. This is Sunday—remember? It was last night I went over to Drew's . . .'

Thinking back, I knew I had felt angry—but it had seemed such a small, isolated incident at the time. Now I wasn't so sure. There had been altogether too many similar 'incidents' over the past few weeks. But how to explain them to my parents?

I had decided not to bother. 'Oh, that's okay,' I had mumbled. 'I'll go out and get something later on. It doesn't matter. I'm not really hungry at the moment. . .'

Now that I had returned, I just stood in the doorway of the living room, staring at the backs of my parents and wanting desperately to confront them with my problem, and yet with a sinking foreknowledge that it would do no good.

I had to grasp the banister as I climbed upstairs. The house had begun to revolve around me, very slowly. I felt sick. My stomach contracted into a hard knot. The incident at McDonald's had completely disoriented me.

I made it to my room, closed the door, and sat down on the edge of my bed, head in hands. What had gone wrong with my world—and who was responsible?

Me? A wave of absurd humour engulfed me. I smiled and thought of *I Was a Victim of Teenage Paranoia* as a likely title for a drive-in movie trade. But the idea only stayed funny for a moment and then I lapsed back into despair. Exhausted, I lay on the bed with my arms clenched behind my head. I stared at the NASA poster on the opposite wall: a beautiful reproduction of a Martian landscape photographed by one of the Viking spacecraft. I often contemplated it after a long and trying day, but that night it didn't help at all.

I made up my mind to skip a few classes the next day

and go down and have a talk with Dr Birch. Whatever was afflicting me had certainly got out of hand: I needed help. Expert advice. Desperately. I had read enough psychology to know that sometimes simple chemical imbalances in the body could produce symptoms similar to my own. My predicament could be something a doctor could fix without recourse to psychiatric treatment.

Persecution paranoia. When it gets really bad you need a referral from your regular doctor to get an appointment with a shrink. I hoped it would never get to that stage, and I drew some consolation from the knowledge that Dr Birch was a straight-talking, no-nonsense sort of person. I liked him. I respected his opinion. He would know what to do and I would soon be back on the rails again and this nightmare behind me—if everything went well.

The Martian poster looked unusually drab—or perhaps that was only the way I saw it. I wondered if this visual trick was yet another manifestation of my peculiar 'condition,' or if the poster had faded just a trifle.

Later, when my parents had retired for the night, I crept downstairs and quietly made myself some supper. The house had ceased its gyrations; I had regained some stability—but not without an enormous effort. My decision to see Dr Birch the following morning may have had something to do with it. Anyway, I no longer felt so desperate.

The kitchen clock showed two-forty. I made a salami and rye sandwich, poured myself a tall glass of milk, and went back upstairs. When I had finished this meagre meal I felt better. The future seemed a possibility. I crawled into bed and slept fitfully.

I woke with a headache and a sense of foreboding.

DR BIRCH is a genial man in his early forties. He has a high, wide forehead and a thatch of fine blond hair. He wears glasses—the old-fashioned horn-rimmed variety—and his soft blue eyes are disarming and carry a hint of mischief which his patients find pleasing. He is always relaxed; nothing ruffles him. He gives the impression that he has all the time in the world. He doesn't bustle you out of his office with a prescription clutched in your hand making you feel you're part of an elaborate assembly line of human beings.

'I learned to stop worrying and rushing around a long time ago,' he once told me. *'Now I take my time, no matter how many people are out there in the waiting room.'* He looks young for his age and he speaks the same language without talking down to me. I had seen him several times before—once when I had a very bad sinus infection which he helped to clear up, again for a throat infection, and of course for my yearly flu shots. But I had never before faced him with a problem of such magnitude. I didn't know where to begin.

He didn't seem unduly worried by my hesitancy. He leaned back in his chair, placed his hands behind his head, and smiled patiently. 'Well, come on, Graeme, what's troubling you this time? You look rather tense.'

I decided there was nothing else to do but to plunge right in. Tell him everything, no matter how crazy it sounded.

'Dr Birch, I think I need to see a shrink.'

His expression didn't alter. His cool eyes studied me casually, waiting for me to go on.

'I mean a *good* one,' I insisted. 'I . . . I think I'm in some kind of trouble and I need help to sort it out. But I don't want my parents to hear about it, if that can be managed. You do understand? I wouldn't like them to be involved, if you could fix it that way . . .'

He said carefully, 'If that's what you think you need, Graeme, then I'm sure it can be arranged. But I suppose you are aware that some psychiatrists feel it necessary to inform the parents if they think the situation is serious enough. You do understand why?'

I nodded. I was still a minor. And I had read enough about modern psychiatric methods to know that sometimes the entire family became involved along with the individual requesting treatment. It was a sore point.

Dr Birch gave me a steady, no-compromise look. 'Maybe it would be a good idea if you told me what's bothering you, and why you think you need to see a psychiatrist.'

I hesitated. It wasn't easy, but eventually I told him. Everything. I just let it all spill out, and I felt such a relief when my strange confession was finished. I left him to make of it what he could. We must have talked for, oh, at least half an hour. He asked me about home, my friends, school; about Annette. How were my grades going? Was I looking forward to university? Was I convinced that an arts course was the best decision? That sort of thing. I went along with him because I knew this was important from his point of view as the family doctor. But I grew increasingly restless. I didn't seem to be getting through to him.

'Look,' I interrupted, 'it isn't anything like that. Really. It's something . . . weird. Like a persecution complex. All these people ignoring me as though I don't exist. You know what I mean. And for the life of me I can't think of anything I've done that should put people off—not total strangers!'

His blue eyes lost their sparkle. He looked suddenly serious. 'I hope you haven't been delving too deeply into pop psychology,' he said carefully. 'A little dabbling with Laing, perhaps? Cooper? Goffman? Fromm?

Szasz? You know what I mean. I feel I should warn you to steer clear of what all the fashionable young schizophrenics are reading if you're as worried as you appear to be.'

The disarming delivery of this advice helped me to relax a little. I shrugged. 'You can't help picking up a little,' I said defensively. 'Eng. lit. is crowded with it these days.'

'I know.'

'And with existentialism and alienation and that sort of thing.'

He sighed. 'That's the difficulty. No wonder young people are beset with problems. They think that—'

I lost patience then. I was not prepared to listen any further to his well-intentioned homilies. My hands were clenched hard in my lap and I glared at him. 'You're not giving me a chance!' I cried, trembling. 'There's something wrong with me! I can feel it. I keep telling you. It may be biological. It may be . . . mental. I just don't know! I can't sleep. I can't eat. My studies are muddled. I can't do *anything* well anymore. The bottom is falling out of my world and I need help. And I need it *now.*'

I think that shook him. He dropped the practised professional mask and drummed his fingers on the desk. He looked thoughtful. 'All right,' he said, 'if that's the way you want it. There's nothing much I can do for you, Graeme. You seem determined to seek out psychiatric help, and from what you've told me I think you're entitled to it. I won't prescribe any tranquillisers because I know how you feel about that sort of medication. Question is, do you think you can hold out long enough until I have arranged a referral?'

I wondered about that. 'How long will it take?' I asked.

'It could take several weeks—'

'But I can't wait that long!'

'I realise that. Look, come in tomorrow morning, nine-thirty sharp, and I'll have ready a letter of referral and—I feel sure—an urgent appointment. I can't, at this stage, tell you when that will be. Does that satisfy you, Graeme?'

It should have, but a niggling doubt remained. It had something to do with Dr Birch. It wasn't that he looked older than I remembered but rather that he seemed unusually pale—like some of the people in his waiting room. I hoped he wasn't unwell. Before I could comment upon his pallor he stood up and ushered me out of his office, a protective arm around my shoulder. I thanked him for giving up so much of his time. He brushed the subject aside. Before he opened the door he paused and gave me a reassuring look. 'Try and take things a little easier until tomorrow morning, will you? Don't push too hard at this thing, whatever it is. You're an intelligent lad. Don't let it drag you under so easily . . .'

His manner convinced me that he was fully aware of the seriousness of my predicament, of my perception of the world. It was reassuring to have gained such an ally, but the relationship threw into dark relief the situation I was in. I really *did* need help. Specialised help.

A shrink.

I DECIDED there would be no point in going to school for the remainder of the day. And besides—I had a feeling that my absence would not be noticed. This, also, seemed part of the growing pattern.

I wandered down Fitzroy Street in the direction of the beach. It was a fine day with a clear sky, but I scarcely noticed. I walked with my head down and my hands thrust angrily into my jacket pockets, oblivious to the bustle of people moving around me.

I stopped at a kiosk on the foreshore and managed to get myself a hot dog without any trouble. I was the only customer, and the middle-aged guy served me in the vague, half-seeing manner I was getting accustomed to.

I crossed the wide stretch of open park that separated the beach from the highway. The towering, neatly tailored palm trees drooped their branches; they seemed curiously lax. Even the shrubs and flower beds looked unusually drab for this time of the year.

The cleaning machines had only just finished clearing the beach of weekend rubbish. The sand stretched out before me, inviting yet curiously drab where it merged with the grey sea.

Grey.

That was my first indication of how alien my world was to become. I remember thinking I'd never seen the sea that colour before, nor the sky, which it so strongly resembled. Why, even the sand looked grey. . .

I studied the horizon carefully. The sea presented a deeper shade of grey than the sand, rolling toward me in gently rounded swells. And where the ocean met the sky there was a very subtle transformation: The drab colour of the sea merged almost imperceptibly with the softer grey of the sky.

Sea.

Sand.

And sky.

The only difference seemed to be a matter of . . . density. I wondered if it was some freak of the weather that had brought about this peculiar situation.

The sun was shining over my right shoulder. I turned around, ready to shield my eyes against the cloudless sky—but what a pallid light struggled fitfully through to me. It was as though a tenuous grey fog had been drawn across the sun. I closed my eyes and blinked—several times. But nothing changed. Was there something wrong with my eyesight?

I looked at the park and thought how easily we come to accept as normal our familiar surroundings, without really questioning them. Although it was early summer the shrubs and flower beds were not the usual riot of colour I would have expected: I saw only pale, pastel hues. The scene might just as well have been painted in watercolours rather than the vibrant reds and blues and yellows I remembered. Even the half-eaten hot dog I held in my hands looked curiously pallid. I threw it away in disgust, much too disturbed to feel guilty about littering.

Nearby I heard the disconsolate cry of seagulls as they whirled and squabbled overhead and scurried for morsels of food along the shoreline. Their cries seemed to echo the crushing loneliness inside me.

I walked a little way down the beach until I found a bench and sat down. With the park at my back I stared out angrily at the monotonous monochrome of sand, sea and sky.

The possibility that my eyesight was also being affected alarmed me more than anything previous. I feared that this was also a result of some obscure emotional disorder.

What emotional disorder? I didn't have any! At least, not that I was aware of. There was only this curious buildup of the most unlikely circumstances, such as—

I remembered reading somewhere that a neurotic is a person who has lost interest in everything but himself . . . but what if outside circumstances, beyond his control, force those considerations upon him?

I felt suddenly too exhausted to think anymore. I curled up on the bench and fell asleep. It was as simple as that. No one bothered me. And when I woke it was late afternoon and a wan sun was settling slowly into a dark grey sea. I felt cold and hungry.

It occurred to me that I hadn't seen a really brilliant sunset in ages. And when I cast my mind back it wasn't only my immediate surroundings that looked drab; there was also Dr Birch's office and also his unusual pallor. I began to wonder if some strange process was leaching all the colour from the world ...

I glanced down at my wristwatch. It was nearly seven p.m. I had been asleep for more than eight hours! I told myself that I must have needed so much rest, but the curious result was that I did not feel refreshed. My head weighed a ton.

'Take it easy,' Dr Birch had advised. Okay: I would go along with him as best I could—let my hallucinations or whatever have their turn but *try and hold on,* no matter what. Until the morning. When I would see Dr Birch again.

'Take it easy ...'

I waited awhile. Until dusk had settled over ocean, beach and park, and the whole world seemed a deeper shade of grey. On the horizon I saw some darker smudges that suggested the presence of gathering clouds, but I could have been wrong. A cold wind blew in from the sea. It was time to go home.

I wondered what kind of a welcome I would receive.

I MADE a lot of noise when I came in the front door. I walked heavily down the hallway and called out, 'Mum?'

I heard her working in the kitchen, humming softly to herself the melody of some old folk song. I think it was 'Barbara Allen.'

I walked into the kitchen and found her busy at the

stove with her back to me. My mother has always been a particularly handsome woman, but I was distressed to see that in the pale light cast by the overhead fluorescents her hair looked grey and her cheeks drained of colour. I remembered the park . . . and the dull grey sand. And I was afraid.

I crept up beside her and said softly in her ear, 'Mum?' My lips almost touched her cheek but she gave no sign that she had heard me. Her eyes were dull, her skin pale.

I took a step back, shaking. I was too astonished to say anything further. I watched her keep on stirring the saucepan on the stove, oblivious to my presence. I could detect the faint aroma of a strongly flavoured meat sauce. I watched her deftly add some more herbs with her free hand while she continued stirring with the other. I wondered what on earth I should do next. Then it came to me.

I remembered Dr Birch's advice. I pulled myself together and took my mother gently by the shoulders and slowly turned her around until she faced me, until she could not help but see me.

I saw a vague, clouded look in her dull eyes. 'It's me, Graeme,' I said, trying to keep the uneasiness out of my voice. 'I'm home. Didn't you hear me come in?'

A half-puzzled expression passed fleetingly across her face. For one wild moment I was afraid that she would not recognise me—her own son!—and that I no longer occupied an important place in her life. And then—

Her expression cleared. The vague look was replaced by a welcoming smile. 'Why, Graeme,' she said, chiding me gently, 'you gave me quite a start, creeping up on me like that . . .'

I was about to say that I had not been 'creeping up on her,' but I thought it better to leave it unsaid. Instead I apologised, and that seemed to please her. But it was like a game in which I was also a spectator, viewing my absurd encounters from a remote distance. For the first time I grew aware of a deep, lingering chill that had settled inside me. I was afraid it would never go away.

'What's . . . for dinner?' I asked casually. Trying to act natural when everything around me was growing unfamiliar.

'Dinner?' The vague look had crept back into her eyes —and her voice. She reminded me of Annette; she did not seem quite 'with it.' Most unusual behaviour for such a gracious and responsible lady. Not like my mother at all.

'Dinner,' she repeated, as though reassuring herself that this was her primary concern. 'Oh, I thought we might have moussaka. Ivan likes it.' So did I, but this hardly seemed worth mentioning.

I looked down at her cutting bench, at the neatly sliced eggplants rolled in flour, ready for frying. Their normally succulent flesh was the colour of yesterday's newspaper. I turned away.

'Did you have . . . a good day?' my mother asked matter-of-factly. She spoke as though the words were of little consequence, stirring the meat sauce slowly and steadily.

I went along with the charade. What else could I do? 'It was okay. Nothing . . . marvellous. I . . . I'll be upstairs if you want me.'

She didn't answer. I left the kitchen and hurried up to my room. I shut the door and sprawled out on the bed, staring up at the ceiling and just letting myself float. Only it didn't work out that way. My thoughts tumbled around in riotous disorder. I desperately wanted to rest, to find a calm at the centre of this nightmarish storm, but this eluded me. What little confidence

I clung to came to me courtesy of Dr Birch. It was the thought of seeing him again in the morning that helped me to hang on; otherwise I might have screamed, just to let out the awful tension I could feel building up inside me. It would be a long night to get through . . .

After a while my attention wandered back to the NASA poster. There was something wrong with it: the Martian landscape was all washed out and featureless; only a pale yellowish tint remained. Gone was the vivid ochre desert and the eerie, pinkish-blue sky.

I rubbed my eyes, but the picture didn't improve. It reminded me of how I had felt down on the beach, how all the colour seemed to be leaching out of the world.

The poster looked ancient. The colours had faded and the magic of gazing upon another world had dissipated. I wondered if, when I woke in the morning, the familiar colours would be restored. I doubted it. Whatever strange malady possessed me seemed to be systematically destroying my perception of the world.

God damn it! I cursed. Maybe Dr Birch was right and it was all in my mind. Everything.

I was cold all over. Deep inside my chest I felt a glacier groan and grind against my heart. I was afraid. I got up and switched on the heater and huddled over it for a few minutes. It made no difference. The cold, the unearthly chill I felt came from within. I couldn't shake it off except by moving around. And I would have to live with it until tomorrow . . . at the least.

Tomorrow: the magic word. Tomorrow I would hurry down and see Dr Birch and he would hand me his letter of referral and an appointment with a shrink who would give me a good going over. He knew how desperate I was.

A while later I heard the front door open and my father's heavy tread in the hallway, curiously muffled.

Late tonight, I thought. He's been working back at the office. No wonder my mother had seemed unhurried preparing dinner.

Scraps of conversation drifted up through the floor. I waited a few minutes longer before I went down to join them. I didn't know what to expect.

They were already seated at the table, facing each other and chatting amiably between mouthfuls. Mother had rearranged her hair and changed into one of her best caftans. I remembered it as the one with the bright orange-and-yellow motif, but now it looked drab. The effect was disquieting.

My father has always been a distinguished-looking man. Impeccably dressed in suits tailored to suit his tall, broad figure. He has dark wavy hair and serious brown eyes. He works for the Department of Civil Aviation, editing an air safety magazine. We are a comfortable, middle-class family, although I'm sure this idea had never occurred to me until then. Suddenly it had become important to identify and hold fast to everything that gave support to my identity.

I stood silently in the doorway for several minutes, watching them like a stranger. They did not notice me. Their conversation was unusually subdued and difficult to follow. My father is by nature an ebullient person and it was strange to hear him speaking in such quiet tones. I watched him pour the wine and gathered that he had returned from a rather hard day's work; some difficulty with a new aerial photographer. He commented on the excellence of the moussaka; mother smiled at the compliment. All this was very familiar, with one extraordinary exception.

There were two lighted candles on the table. And no place had been set for me.

I didn't panic. I remembered Dr Birch's advice. I felt

distanced, isolated—like someone watching an intimate stage play with only one person in the audience: myself.

I walked over to the table. They continued to ignore me. And I saw that my father's hair, which had always been dark and highlighted by some wisps of grey around the sides and temple, now lacked brilliance. His face was as pale as Mother's. Their flesh was the colour of a corpse.

Moving like someone in a dream I eavesdropped on their barely audible conversation. I heard my mother remark something to the effect that she 'wondered where I was' but that she expected me to 'phone in fairly soon.'

That really shook me. I was having increasing difficulty catching their conversation and I wondered if my hearing was being affected by the malaise I had contracted. I had no choice but to go along with events and see what happened. I could scarcely hear the clatter of cutlery and the clink of wine glasses against plates. My mother listened attentively to my father. Occasionally I caught a glimpse of concern, of genuine worry, but it soon disappeared.

I walked slowly around the table, watching them in detail, like a movie director making a long, lingering pan with his camera . . . or a hunter stalking an elusive prey. I felt betrayed.

'I'm here,' I called out, so loud that I felt the walls must have shaken. 'Can't you see me? Can't you hear me? Don't you even want to know me?'

They did not indicate, by even the slightest flicker in their eyes or the faintest movement of their facial muscles, that they were aware of my presence in the room; the flow of conversation went on without pause.

I was too afraid to try and reach out and touch them, for fear they would not react. It had worked earlier, with mother, in the kitchen, but this time I just couldn't bring myself to do it. There had to be some other way.

I wandered out into the kitchen, dazed and unable to comprehend this latest turn of events. It was getting more difficult every moment to grasp the mystery that surrounded me.

There was some moussaka left over in the casserole, a little rice—but no greens. I helped myself to some of these remnants without any real enthusiasm and sat down at the table. I ate morosely. The food was flavourless, not at all like Mother's cooking. But I finished what I had dished out and poured myself a glass of milk. It didn't taste of *anything*. I left it unfinished.

I felt the shakes coming on again and remembered what Dr Birch had said about tranquillisers. Sure, I didn't like pill popping, but I wondered how I was going to see the night out without some kind of sleeping pill.

The hasty meal settled heavily in my stomach. The house was suddenly oppressive. I felt unwanted, unwelcome in my own home. I had to break out.

I hurried upstairs, grabbed my jacket, checked my wallet to make sure I had enough cash, then beat a hasty exit. I slammed the door soundly behind me.

I TOOK a bus to the Valhalla Cinema in Richmond. I didn't volunteer my fare. The driver did not seem to care. The night weighed heavily upon me. Street lights struggled to pierce a darkness deeper than I had ever experienced and the headlights of passing cars seemed to be operating on half power. And the sound of traffic was strangely muted. I saw no stars, I felt sure there was a clear sky overhead, but an impenetrable canopy somehow hid the heavens.

I got off the bus and walked a few blocks down Victoria Street and arrived at the theatre. The first movie was about to begin. I glanced quickly at the board, saw it was an old favourite, and hurried inside.

I didn't bother to buy a ticket and no one challenged me. I was beginning to take advantage of my strange new life and the way people ignored me. I think I would have welcomed being pulled up, but I walked casually through the doorway without anyone interfering. I selected a seat in the centre, twelve rows from the front —my favourite position—and settled down to wait for an usher's arm to fall on my shoulder. It didn't. I was now as 'invisible' outside my own home as I had been inside. The thought made me shiver. I barely had time to consider the implications before the film began.

It was Cocteau's *Beauty and the Beast*—in glorious black and white. I must have seen it, oh, at least seven or eight times previously; but I find something new to enjoy every time I see it. The print was badly worn and the sound track was poor, although I couldn't be sure if this constant fading of the actors' voices was a consequence of the old print or of my own peculiar hearing defect which had only recently developed. Everything seemed so far away . . .

For an hour and a half I let myself be caught up once again in Cocteau's magical world. I didn't have time to feel insecure; I was too deeply immersed in the wonder before me.

The film came to an end and the house lights went up. There were only a few people in the cinema; some moved out into the foyer for coffee and small talk. I stayed in my seat, hunched down and reluctant to let the outside world intrude. I held fast in my mind the final image of the young prince in the film, miraculously transformed from his beastly spell into a handsome—but not quite convincing—hero, rising effortlessly with his Beauty into a heavenly sky. Powerful stuff.

I waited anxiously for the second feature to begin (you always get your money's worth at the Valhalla). I was eager to lose myself for another few hours. I reckoned it would be close to midnight by the time I arrived home...

The lights dimmed.

I had not checked out the lobby poster to see what the second film would be; I had been in too much of a hurry when I arrived. But I was delighted when it turned out to be another favourite, although of more recent vintage, which I had seen only twice before: *Aces High*. I was quickly caught up again in the magic of cinema, watching the remarkable evocation of the hapless, helpless lives of the doomed fighter aces in the First World War—an enormous step away from the romantic heroics of Errol Flynn and his *Dawn Patrol* (which I had also enjoyed). But that had been another time and another place. The world had changed and so had the attitude of some people toward the horrors of war.

The film was supposed to be in colour—at least that was how I remembered it: the extraordinary use of the colour camera in the aerial dogfights over France, in the muddy fields below, and through the forced good humour of the barrack-room scenes. But the images I now saw were muddy watercolours, and as with the previous film I had to strain to catch the actors' words. This time I was convinced that it wasn't a faulty print.

The programme finished at eleven-twenty. I took my time walking back to the bus stop and, as I had anticipated, it was close to midnight when I arrived home.

As soon as I stepped inside the front door I was gripped by the same uneasiness I had felt before. I felt as though I did not *belong* there. And yet it was my home...

I remembered the sleeping pills. As much as I disliked

the idea of taking sedatives, I knew that I needed a good night's sleep—desperately. I wanted to be alert when I saw Dr Birch in the morning. So I went into the bathroom and opened the medicine cabinet. I found a small bottle I had seen many times before and read the label carefully.

MRS DRURY. TAKE ONE OR TWO
TABLETS BEFORE RETIRING.

I poured myself a glass of water and took three, just to make sure. Then I went back to my room and crawled into bed. Only the weak glow of my bed lamp held the shadows at bay. I had not listened to the news all day and I wondered if the city was operating on reduced power because of some industrial crisis.

I reached out with a heavy hand and angled the lamp so that it shone directly upon the Martian poster. By now the familiar landscape had all but disappeared. It, too, looked like something left over from the First World War: a vague pencil rendering with a few daubs of halftone. But no colours. No colour at all...

I switched off the bed lamp and lay sprawled out in the darkness, feeling a pleasant heaviness begin to penetrate my mind and body. I knew I would soon be asleep, that the sedatives were working, and for this relief I was indeed most thankful. I relaxed and let the Valium or whatever it was keep up the good work. I was beginning to feel deliciously drowsy. My last conscious thought was that perhaps I had overdone the pills; two would have been ample.

I WOKE with a heavy, clouded head and with no feeling in my limbs. *Too much,* I thought. *I overdid it.* And for what seemed a long time I lay quite still, unable to move. It was only with a considerable effort that I managed to keep my eyes open; focusing them presented another problem.

So much for sedatives. Next time—

But there wouldn't be a next time, I told myself. Dr Birch would see to that. And if not he, then the shrink would take care of me. No more sleeping pills and feeling afraid of my own parents.

I looked down groggily at my wristwatch. With an effort I saw that it read eleven-fifteen.

That jolted me awake. I should have been down at the doctor's two hours ago!

I tried to sit up. The room whirled around me and took its own time coming to a stop.

Why hadn't I been called? Mother usually attended to me when I overslept and looked as if I would be late for school.

Gone too far, I thought in my muddled state. *Can't trust anyone anymore. Only myself. And Dr Birch.*

I managed to sit up. God, but I felt awful. I knew I wasn't up to leaping out of bed in a hurry, but I tried—and made a frightful mess of it. I collapsed into an awkward heap on the carpet, feeling very silly. I waited until the room had stopped its hurdy-gurdy antics and then crawled over to the armchair where my clothes were draped. I managed to get dressed, moving slowly and clumsily.

My head felt as though it was stuffed with enough cotton to burst it. There was no ache, only a clogged-up feeling. I struggled along. I pulled on a T-shirt and then my matching jeans and jacket and managed to get into my sneakers. After that I felt better. I could even stand up, swaying a little and grabbing hold of the back of the chair for support. When I could see things more clearly and had more confidence in my movements, I made my way cautiously downstairs.

The house was deserted. Father had long since left for work and mother would be either out shopping or visiting neighbours. And they had *both* neglected to wake me. Why?

I concentrated on the business in hand. I let breakfast wait; the important thing was to get down to Dr Birch—fast. Before he took his lunch break.

His clinic was located at the end of our street. I think I must have run all the way—weaving this way and that like a drunken fool in my giddy haste. It was a wonder that I did not injure myself in that wild gallop. I opened the heavy glass doors and stumbled inside, gasping for breath. I reckon I must have looked a sight.

The waiting room was filled with the usual regulars.

I leaned on the reception desk and tried to attract the attention of the nurse. She was busy checking files.

'Miss,' I said, breathing heavily. 'I have an appointment with Dr Birch. I . . . I'm late. I was supposed to be here at nine-thirty. I, ah, sort of . . . overslept. I'm sorry. Is he in? I have to pick up a letter of referral or something like that . . .'

My voice trailed away. She wasn't listening. Head down, her attention remained firmly fixed on the neat stack of file cards on her desk. She was shuffling them carefully as though she was looking for something that had been lost or mislaid.

Only then did I become aware of the unusual silence in the waiting room. Not a cough, not a wheeze, not even a wary shifting of a buttock in its chair. Silence.

'Miss,' I called out. 'I have to see Dr Birch!'

Again she did not respond. She remained unruffled in spite of my outburst. I looked around. Not a single person in the room had looked up. Some read magazines, others stared vacantly into space. All of them bore the same dreadful pallor.

I pounded on the desk with both fists, letting out my anger and frustration. 'Miss! Will you please let me see Dr Birch? *This is urgent.* He's expecting me . . .'

She should have been outraged by the liberties I had taken. She could have screamed that a patient was molesting her. But no—the only indication she gave that she had heard my tirade was to raise her head just a trifle and give me a vague look.

There it was again! I felt like reaching out and grabbing hold of her shoulders and shaking her like a rag doll until she acknowledged my existence—but I remembered the doctor's advice and quickly stifled the impulse.

'Miss,' I said gently, and lifted her chin so that she was looking me straight in the eyes. 'Please.' Louder this time. 'Will you listen to me? I have to see Dr Birch. It's . . . it's a matter of life and death. I *have* to see him. Now. He's expecting me.'

The vague look slowly gave way to one of recognition. Her lips parted. She hesitated, then said, 'What did you say . . . your name was?'

'I didn't.' Her face bore the same deathly pallor as everyone else in the room. 'It's Graeme Drury. You have a card for me in there.' I indicated the stack in front of her. 'I saw Dr Birch yesterday. He asked me to come back this morning and—'

'Dr Birch, you said?'

She was starting to look vague again.

'Yes. He was to write me a letter of referral. He was also supposed to make an appointment for me with, er, another doctor—'

'A letter,' she repeated, echoing my words from what seemed a great distance away, yet I was so close I could see where her mascara had smeared.

'That's right,' I said angrily. 'That's what I'm here for. That's what I've been trying to tell you. Now could you please—'

But she wasn't listening. Only for a moment did she allow her attention to wander to the door that bore Dr Birch's nameplate; then she lowered her head and resumed shuffling the file cards.

I was dumbfounded. I had felt sure she was about to get up and knock on that all-important door, but now I saw that I had lost her attention—what little of it I had managed to grasp.

I straightened up and without another word marched straight across the room and pounded heavily on the door. My efforts were reproduced as a muffled thud. I could hardly believe my own ears.

'Dr Birch! Dr Birch!' I called out, hammering away at the wooden panel. 'It's me—Graeme Drury. I've come for my letter! Can you hear me, Dr Birch?'

No answer.

I hammered and yelled some more. It helped drive the anger and humiliation out of my system. Exhausted, I leaned heavily against the door, my head whirling. For a moment I almost blacked out. I wanted to vomit, my fear was so great.

Behind me the nurse continued playing with her file cards. The people in the waiting room were mute and unsmiling. Beyond the windows the sun shone on a pallid world that went on about its business—and I was *alone*.

'Dr Birch?' I called out, weakly this time. My energy had been spent. Everything seemed to be slipping away from me—mind, body, *me*—the personality that was *I*. I was desperate but exhausted. I didn't know what to do next.

The door opened. I almost stumbled and fell through

into the room beyond. I steadied myself and took a step back instead. Dr Birch stood in the doorway, his right hand holding the door open. But he was not looking at me. He was looking *past* me, or rather *through* me. There was a mild frown of annoyance on his ghostly face.

'Miss Pilgrim,' he said—I could barely hear him—'did I hear some kind of disturbance out here?'

The girl looked up and shook her head. 'No, doctor. Nothing out here.'

He shook his head. 'That's strange.' And before I had recovered enough to try and grasp his attention he had closed the door in my face.

I let my hands hang impotent at my sides. Why bother? No matter how hard I tried to make my presence felt, I was convinced I was wasting my time. The process or whatever was too far advanced: I was very neatly being removed from all contact with reality.

I looked again at the people in the waiting room. The women wore faded print dresses, the men drab suits and pullovers. As I remembered, the walls and ceiling of the room had been painted a relaxing pale blue, but now they were an ominous shade of grey.

There came a roaring in my ears.

Hold on, I told myself. *You must hold on. Until this thing is finished. Until the process is . . . complete.*

The room tilted at a crazy angle. It was difficult for me to breathe. I leaned against the closed door until I regained some control over my body—then I made a bolt for the outside door. My only thought was to get away from the place as fast as possible, and perhaps come to grips with my predicament in a less hostile environment.

I felt better outside. A little warmth filtered down from the wan sun and I found I could breathe easier. I wandered—aimlessly. Trying to forget the fear and get my mind functioning properly again. What to do next?

I lost track of my surroundings. I knew the St Kilda and Elwood area well enough; we had lived there for three years. So I wasn't worried. But when I finally came to a stop, leaned back against a high brick fence, and surveyed my surroundings, for a moment I thought I was lost.

I couldn't have walked very far; my wristwatch indicated it was just after noon. It was the area I had reached that I found difficult to recognise. All the buildings were a uniform grey, and the cars that flashed quietly by wore muted pastels. The few pedestrians I saw were darker blurs against the pervading greyness. There was a park opposite. I plunged my hands into my jacket pocket and crossed the street.

The park was as drab as the one down by the beach—but I recognised the layout. The space-age playground no longer screeched at me with its brilliant red and yellow and blue domes and swings and slides; the colours were as hushed as those I had seen elsewhere, and the beds of flowers were lifeless. An eerie silence overlay my world. And how visually monotonous it had become!

I felt a faint breeze stir against my cheek and turned in that direction. I knew where I was—I even imagined I could sense the salt tang of the sea in my nostrils, but that was an illusion. The beach was close. I began walking that direction, perhaps hoping to find in solitude what had eluded me in company.

I remember arriving at the beach and stretching out, facedown, in the strange grey sand. I dug my fingers into it, searching for a warmth that wasn't there. I remember crying, and not feeling embarrassed or ashamed, simply relieved. There was no one around to see me or to care. If there had been then I think I would have wept for joy. The more I thought about it, the more likely it seemed that I was no longer a part of the world I had known since childhood, that I had been displaced from it by some mysterious process I could not understand, and for reasons that were equally confusing.

After a while I lay on my back and watched the grey gulls wheeling overhead. Then I turned my gaze out to sea, let it wander across the dull grey waves until they merged almost imperceptibly with the drab sky. The tireless sound of the surf was denied to me—that, and the sound of the gulls and the wind that tugged at my hair.

Several hours had passed since I had fled Dr Birch's clinic. Now that I was calmer I tried to consider the future rationally. How far would this thing, this *process*, continue?

I feared for my future, for my life, for everything I had ever known and loved—and there was no one I could turn to for help. The incident with Dr Birch had proved that point beyond any doubt whatsoever.

Was I really insane? A victim of grossly distorted hallucinations and completely out of touch with the real world? Or had I been singled out for some kind of experiment, by intelligences alien or otherwise, the nature of which I could not comprehend?

But why me?

I got up and brushed sand off my jeans. And I made a startling discovery. In retrospect it was damn near apocalyptic, but at the time I could only wonder why I hadn't noticed it before . . .

I was surrounded by merging shades of grey, but while the world seemed to have been systematically drained of colour, the blue of my jeans screamed at me.

I raised my hands and studied them. I saw the blue veins, close to the surface—a genetic inheritance from my mother's side of the family—and the healthy skin.

I had not changed.

Whatever mysterious process was at work, it had left me untouched! I felt like a vibrant, full-colour figure stranded in a drab world of grey.

My spirit picked itself up. Now it seemed that I had positive proof that the world around me was undergoing a strange metamorphosis from which I had somehow become exempt. This realisation brought forth a further question: How far did the greyworld extend? I decided to find out.

But first I needed something to eat. I thought of going home and grabbing what I could find in the kitchen, without bothering mother. So I hurried back up Fitzroy Street, hardly noticing the busy midday crowd (drab little people with washed-out faces and faded grey clothes).

Curiously, I was never jostled or bumped into by anyone, despite my head-down and hands-in-pocket attitude. Sometimes I felt a surge of power and I likened myself to a full-colour, three-dimensional creature parading through a grotesque gallery of faded, old-fashioned human beings. Oh, my condition was dangerous, all right, and I had to work hard to keep my mind on an even keel. It wasn't easy.

I arrived home, swung open the gate, and walked up the cobbled path, averting my eyes from the dreary garden which had been my mother's pride. I fumbled in my pockets for my front-door key . . . It wasn't there. Nor was my wallet. I had fled the house in such a rush that I had left both behind.

I raised my right hand . . . then let it fall. What was the use of banging on the door? I didn't expect my summons would be heard. Better to sneak in by the back door.

The back door was locked from inside. Mother had gone out and bolted it as was customary. I tried the windows, driven almost to desperation not so much by my mounting hunger as by increasing frustration.

Every window was locked. That, also, was to be expected. My mother is always particular about locking up, as she calls it, before going out. There was no way for me to get inside—unless I smashed a window.

For a fraction of a second I raised my hand and was about to do just that—in a fit of temper. But I lowered the fist. What was the use? I got the peculiar feeling that I no longer belonged here, that the house was effectively closed to me.

Dazed, I took a step back from the window I had been about to break. If I did not find food somewhere I would starve. That much was obvious. I had not eaten anything since my meagre supper in the early hours of the morning. If I was doomed to live out the rest of my life in this peculiar fashion then I had best make some effort to come to grips with it.

I went back to Fitzroy Street. The sound of traffic was a muted hum. I found a supermarket and went in. I helped myself to a small carton of milk, two bread rolls with sesame seeds, some butter, a short length of Polish sausage—and two apples. On my way out I detoured through the kitchenware section and picked up a small, serrated knife. Then I walked calmly out through the checkout and filled a large paper bag with my acquisitions.

No one challenged me. I would have welcomed it if they had. But it was the same as it had been at the theatre: I just wasn't visible to these people.

I found myself a seat in the park and began assembling a hasty lunch. The food was virtually tasteless. It was like chewing dough. I almost gagged. I couldn't detect a trace of garlic in the sausage, but I forced it and the bread rolls down because I knew I needed nourishment. The milk was a thick, glutinous liquid without any flavour. Only the apples possessed a very faint bitter-sweet aftertaste and I bit into them hungrily.

I dumped the remains of my lunch in a litter bin and then set off in the direction of the city—a dark silhouette of grey rising in the distance. I had resolved to step out and discover the perimeter of my greyworld. I desperately needed to find a point where familiar colours reappeared. And I had no idea how far I would need to travel . . .

I rode a tram as far as Flinders Street. I didn't offer my fare to the conductor because I knew he wouldn't be interested. I walked blithely through the railway station entrance, equally confident that no one would stop me. And I was right.

Melbourne was as depressingly grey as my St Kilda surroundings, with the exception that there were no pallid flowers to accentuate the strangeness—only tall, ugly buildings towering over me like gravestones, and the drab and faded clothes of the pedestrians. The familiar bustle and roar of city traffic was audible to me as only a kind of stammering murmur.

I waited and then boarded a train that would take me to the nearby hills. The Dandenong Ranges were only an hour away, and I settled down in a corner seat by a window and waited for the train to get moving. I was impatient to see how far the greyworld persisted, and yet afraid of what I might find.

I watched the dreary suburbs unfold before me like a strip of faded motion-picture film. It was a city devoid of colour, of warmth, of any sort of life I could recognise. The greyness stretched as far as I could see, crowding the horizon and unrolling toward me like relentless fog.

My heart fell when we reached the open country and the train began the leisurely climb through the Dandenong foothills toward Belgrave. The landscape was all washed out, the same pall of gloom hung over the Ranges and showed no sign of dissipating.

Belgrave was the end of the line. I got off and boarded a bus that took me a further 10 kms to Monbulk, a small town nestling on the far side of the hills. The road was long and narrow and winding; a well-known and much advertised scenic drive. But as the vehicle wound its way through the hills I grew increasingly depressed. I missed the dazzling floral displays that the area was noted for. The greyworld had swallowed up the entire area. Sometimes a flight of birds would swoop across the sky, unrecognisable now that they had been robbed of their brilliant plumage. Only the hardy kookaburra looked familiar in his dress of grey and white, but even he was subdued.

The bus rounded a corner and entered Monbulk. I could now look out across more than 30 kms of what had once been green countryside, with distant mountains looming on the horizon. But nowhere saw I a solitary splash of vibrant colour to impeach the greyworld. It reached out to the mountains and, for all I knew, probably beyond. *Perhaps throughout the entire world.* It was a thought that filled me with dread . . .

If the greyness and the awful silence girdled the world, why had I been singled out to bear witness to a tragedy that everyone else, pale-faced, seemed to be taking for granted?

My worst suspicions had been confirmed and I was anxious to get back to the city before dusk. So I waited and took the return trip, counting off the kilometres so that the journey seemed to take twice as long.

I felt a little more secure when I was again on board the train heading back to Melbourne. I settled down to the dreary monotony of the starting and stopping of the train, the doors sliding open, and people getting on and off—pale ghosts now in a deepening greyworld—and I asked myself again: Was I truly seeing the real world, or an eerie projection of my own disturbed mind?

I remembered the conundrum posed by the ancient Chinese sage Chuang-tzu: How he dreamed one day that he was a butterfly, happily flitting about and enjoying life without knowing who he was. Then he woke and found that he was indeed Chuang-tzu. And he asked himself, 'Did I dream I was a butterfly, or did the butterfly dream he was Chuang-tzu?'

Something like that. I was beginning to feel like that old fellow. Was it possible that my life, up to now, had been no more than a dream, that the reality I had known had been but a pretence, and that I was about to embark upon some mysterious metamorphosis?

If you take a word—any simple, ordinary, everyday word—and repeat it over to yourself often enough you will soon discover that it loses all meaning; sheer repetition robs any word of our familiarity with it. Could it be so with life itself?

I though these were very wild, very bold thoughts for someone like myself, who had never worried much before about existence. And they were not uplifting. As I walked out of Flinders Street station and viewed again the sickly wasteland of the city, I wondered if I was indeed mad, or if I had been displaced from an older order of reality . . . and placed in another.

I boarded the first tram that would take me home.

Home. Panic took hold of me and I remembered I would have to get back to the house before my father, so that I could slip in after him when he opened the front door. I doubted if I would be able to gain entry by any other means.

I reached the gate with twenty minutes to spare. I crept around the back of the house. Through the kitchen window I saw the pale wraith of my mother preparing dinner in the kitchen. I found myself unable to move, and stood there in a state of trance until, dimly, I heard a soft swish that indicated the front gate had swung open. The sound was almost too faint to register —like a soft pencil drawn across a sheet of textured paper. But a desperate part of my mind had remained alert, despite my trance, waiting for it. I hurried around to the front of the house.

Father did not notice me. That was now not unusual. I waited breathlessly while he fumbled for his keys. The lock turned and the door swung open. Without hesitation I slipped in behind him before he could close it with his customary careless backward swing.

Inside, the house was dank and grey, like a sepulchre. Outside, a nacreous twilight was developing. I felt very much alone . . . and afraid.

The dining table was set for two.

Father put down his coat and briefcase before going out into the kitchen to be welcomed by Mother. Their conversation was inaudible.

My legs felt as though they were filled with water. It took an effort to make them move. I groped my way upstairs. The banister felt curiously smooth—almost viscous—as though it had recently been dusted with a fine, dry lubricant. It was my first experience of what I came to call the 'interface,' but at the time I did not realise the significance under my sliding fingers.

I needed my own room. Surely the friendly, familiar surroundings would enable me to figure out what to do next.

But I was wrong. My own room was as alien to me as the rest of the house. The bed, the desk, the shelves filled with books and the stereo all seemed to belong to another world, another person. Not to me. Not to Graeme Drury.

The bed was unmade, just as I had left it. And there wasn't a trace of colour anywhere. Here, in the fortress of my own room, the mysterious process had worked as industriously as it had in the outside world.

I thought, *I no longer belong here.* I also wondered if I ever had. The concept made my scalp prickle.

What could I do? Where could I sleep? Certainly not here. Downstairs, then. On the couch? When my parents had retired for the night I could creep down with some spare blankets, fix myself a tasteless supper, and then try to get some sleep.

The idea seemed plausible—but as I made my way cautiously downstairs and experienced again the curiously viscous nature of the banister, I realised that I had to get away from the house. The overwhelming rejection of my presence in my own home was frightening. To be ignored by strangers and friends was one thing, but by my own flesh and blood . . .!

I looked down at the dinner table set for two, then through the kitchen doorway where my parents were conversing amiably enough. My eyes filled with tears of frustration—and I fled. I flung open the door and ran out into the awful greyworld, determined to find somewhere else to spend the night. I had no idea where I should go, or even what I should do next. I was *lost*.

Whatever happened, I would have to hold on. I was convinced now that no human hand would reach out to help me, that I was more isolated than any creature on God's earth.

I WANDERED aimlessly through the transfigured night. Pale streetlamps shed a pallid glow. Eventually I found myself standing on the footpath outside Annette's house, staring glumly at the windows.

Well, why not?

Some feeling had drawn me there. What could I hope to find inside her house that had been denied me elsewhere? A place that was not as painfully close as my own home, and with someone to whom I felt closer than my parents, though in a different way?

My luck was in. The back door was open—it was a warm night—and the porch light was on. I heard popular music playing on the family stereo. The sound was so faint it might just as well have come from the other side of the street.

I took a deep breath and stepped boldly inside. I would have felt enormous relief to have been recognised, but I knew this was a forlorn hope.

The family were seated around the large kitchen dining table. They were busy with their meal and talking with great animation, the way some large families do.

Annette was the youngest of the three girls. Jennifer and Drusilla were twins—dark hair, slender, and very good-looking. Jenny worked as a secretary to some industrial firm. Drusilla did the same with some chemical company whose name I've forgotten. Both were very much career oriented. Annette was . . . different. A dreamer. She had always seemed poised on the edge of a far more adventurous life than her older sisters—I think it was this very quality which had attracted me to her— and she was not quite sure what to do with her life. We had talked a lot about it; I felt much the same way. Her father was someone very high up in governmental circles. Her mother was active in local community aid and welfare work. Nice people. Gregarious and helpful. I liked them. But Annette was the deep thinker, and also the most considerate in her relationships with other people. We were very close. She was good company and never made any demands upon our relationship. A pang of regret assailed me: Had I lost her too?

I walked slowly around the big table staring intently into each pair of eyes in turn, searching for some flicker of recognition. But their faces—even Annette's—wore the same dreadful pallor I had seen everywhere else.

Ghosts.

Or did I have it the wrong way around? Could it be that it was I—?

The smell of cooking was missing. The bustling conversation of the family, with all its crisscrossing threads, was only a murmur on the threshold of my hearing. Moment by moment the real world—or what remained of it—was retreating.

When I had reassured myself that I had in no way trespassed upon their privacy, I proceeded to help myself to a few slices of tasteless roast beef that I carved from the platter on a nearby buffet. I grabbed some leftover baked potatoes—which I knew would be equally tasteless—and wandered out of the ghostly kitchen. I sat in the living room with my plate on my lap and got the food down. The stereo played whimsically in the background. Later, I helped myself to a cup of coffee. The coffee tasted warm, and that was all.

Later I found myself standing in Annette's room. Her bed was unmade. Some clothes were scattered across the carpet, together with paperback books and magazines and unfinished schoolwork. I smiled. Oh, this was Annette's room, all right. No question about it . . .

I sat down on the edge of the bed and brooded. The coffee grew cold in my hands and I put it aside.

I must have lost all track of time—something I had

been experiencing too frequently of late—for when I looked up suddenly I saw Annette was in the room.

It gave me quite a start. I hadn't heard her come in—how could I, with my hearing no longer reliable? I got up from the bed and was about to say something, to apologise, when I realised that it wasn't necessary. She didn't know I was there.

She shut her door and switched on the overhead light. The room seemed unnaturally dim. I glanced at her bedside clock. It was eight-thirty.

I watched her cross over to her desk, idly stopping to pick up some pieces of discarded underwear from the carpet.

I said gently, 'Annette?' As if my presence, as if my affection could somehow bridge the abyss that kept us apart.

She tidied her desk.

I walked up behind her and said again, louder this time, 'Annette? It's me, Graeme.'

She went on with her work.

I reached out to grasp her shoulders. My hands clasped her
—and slipped
—slid away.

I could not hold her. I could not even touch her! My hands made contact only with the same viscous surface I had felt before on the banister back home.

And there was . . . a tension between us. It was almost palpable. As though an invisible barrier separated us—some sort of interface between *her* world and *mine*.

She switched on the desk lamp and sat down. She opened a book on medieval history, yawned, and with an I-must-get-this-done-tonight expression proceeded to study.

I turned away, shaking. There was an old-fashioned

armchair by the window. I sat down in it, my head spinning. How much more? I asked. How much longer? Where would it all end?

I kept watching Annette. I gathered together every ounce of my will and tried to call out wordlessly across the room. *Annette, you have to hear me! I need you. I need help. I'm so lost . . .*

I kept this up until my head hurt. Then I went over to her again, hoping perhaps that mere proximity would add weight to my unspoken plea.

She had her head down, studying the printed page. I leaned my hands on the desk and hovered slightly to her left. I forged all my despair into what I imagined was a fiery psychic spear, shaped it, and hurled it into her mind . . . and her heart.

Annette—can't you hear me? Have you, too, forgotten me so soon? Help me. For God's sake—help me!

My hands were shaking and I grasped the edge of the desk firmly. I felt weak and dizzy. Any moment I expected to topple over . . .

Something happened. Annette looked up. There was a faraway look in her eyes. She held up a pencil and butted it firmly against her teeth. She frowned. A look of uneasiness crept into her eyes.

I took a step back, breathing heavily. Had I managed to get through to her, or had some other thought disturbed her concentration?

She got up from the desk and went out into the hall. I followed her. She picked up the phone and dialled a number—*my* number. There was an expression of concern on her face while she waited for the call to be answered.

And it was. She dipped her head when she talked and I couldn't make out a word of what she said. She spoke for perhaps thirty seconds and then hung up. There was a curious expression in her eyes. She gave a little shrug and went back to her room. I stared at the phone for a moment longer, then hurried after her. I slipped into her room just before she closed the door.

She went back to her desk and resumed her studies.

I collapsed in the armchair in a fit of despair. I had no way of knowing if my thoughts and feelings had actually reached her in some way and motivated her phone call, or if she had simply followed some intuition of her own.

I felt defeated. I didn't know what to do next. And I think that some kind of mental circuit breaker must have cut into my thoughts and saved me from a mounting hysteria, because the next thing I remember is waking suddenly from a deep sleep.

I sat up with a start. The room was not yet in darkness. Annette was in bed, reading by the light of a lamp on her bedside table. The time was eleven-fifteen. She wore summer-weight pyjamas and she had untied her long hair from a ponytail so that it was spread very attractively around her shoulders. Despite her dreadful pallor she looked achingly beautiful.

I could not move. I sat there watching. Abruptly she yawned, put aside the paperback novel she had been reading, reached over, and switched off the lamp. The room was plunged into darkness.

For a moment I was terrified. I had not been prepared for this sudden change in my surroundings. I tried to grasp the arms of the chair, but the upholstery felt oily under my hands and I could not get a firm grip. Again, the mysterious interface. I sat with my mouth open, heart hammering, staring into the darkness.

Slowly my eyes adjusted. I saw a faint glow creeping in through the curtains from the streetlamps outside. I could just make out Annette's features. She was lying on her left side, facing me. And although she was asleep her face wore a disturbed expression.

I could have reached out and touched her, my chair was so close. But I hesitated. The wan light gave her face a ghastly look. I turned quickly away.

I don't know how long I sat there, unmoving. I do remember that at no stage did I feel cold, and that struck me as rather odd, because at this time of the year the nights often grew cold.

I was cold *inside*, all right: That great lump of fear never left me for a moment. Eventually I fell asleep again. There wasn't much else I could do; the burden of so much thinking weighed me down.

Sometime during the night I walked in my sleep. I must have been dreaming and felt unbearably lonely. When I woke in the early hours of the morning I found myself lying beside her, on top of the bedclothes. She was still fast asleep.

I kept quite still. I wondered if I had been drawn to her during the night in search of a warmth and comfort I could not find within myself. I felt nothing underneath me. It was as though my body were supported on a cushion of air; I had no contact with the bedclothes, and there was no sensation of a bed yielding to my weight.

The interface again?

For a while I was too afraid to move, lest I disturb this strange equilibrium. Out of the corner of my eye I saw Annette stir. She sat up groggily and reached over to turn off the alarm. It must have shrilled, but I had not heard it. She slumped back on her pillow and lay there with a worried expression. She allowed herself another ten minutes to come to terms with the new day, then she got up.

She took off her pyjamas and stretched, yawning.

And there was nothing prurient in the way I watched her. I had seen her naked before, but never like this. A beautiful body: small breasts, full hips, a slender waist and long legs. But now she was like a marble statue without a sheen. She stood poised on tiptoe for a moment, her languid arms stretched above her head and her image etched deep in my mind. Then she sighed, and broke the spell, and pulled on the Japanese happi coat I had given her for her birthday. It was a lightweight dressing gown with wide oriental sleeves, and it came down to midthigh. I remembered it as being bright red, with a vivid-yellow dragon motif. Now it was the colour of woodsmoke, and the motif was barely distinguishable. She tied the cord loosely around her waist and wandered sleepily out into the hall. Her face was sullen, and I wondered what bad dreams she had had, and if my presence had in any way affected them.

I managed to sit up. When I swung my legs over the side of the bed and set them down on the floor they seemed to give just a fraction under my weight.

I stood up. My legs were shaky. I took a few hesitant steps. I felt as though I were walking on some kind of trampoline. It seemed that overnight I had lost physical contact with the 'outside' world. I wondered rather objectively what new developments awaited me. I felt curiously detached. Numb. I would by now have welcomed an end to my nightmare.

I made my way over to the window, getting accustomed to the slippery interface that now separated me from the 'outside' world. It was rather like a sailor trying to find his 'land legs' when he returned home.

I could not draw the curtains; they would not respond to my touch. I gave up and peered out through a chink along the bottom. The dreary greyworld was all I could see.

I held up my hands. They glared back at me, vibrant with life as the colour of flesh should be. The blue of my denims was a blinding affirmation of my self. This much, at least, had not changed. I took a deep breath, then called out: 'Hello—is anyone there? Can anyone hear me?' And I heard my own voice ring out sharp and clear. But as for the rest . . .

The silence was complete. There was not even a ringing in my ears. The absence of any kind of sound was absolute.

I knew I was only tormenting myself by remaining so close to Annette. The more I hung around familiar faces and places, the more lonely I became, the more deeply I regretted my loss.

I waited until Annette returned from the bathroom. Her face had a freshly scrubbed look but the pallor remained. I watched her dress, conscious of the ache in my chest. 'Good-bye, Annette,' I said softly. There was no need to shout; she would never hear me. Not now. Not ever. I would have given anything to have reached out and held her, however briefly, before I left—but I accepted that this was impossible. The interface saw to that.

She shivered suddenly, as though someone had walked over her grave. Could that someone have been me?

I paused long enough for a lingering look into her dull eyes before I left.

I THINK I must have run—stumbled—half a block in blind panic before I came to my senses.

The pain of being so close and yet so far removed from Annette had sent me fleeing from her house. And it was only when I stopped to draw breath that I remembered I had not even tried to open the front door—

I had run right through it.

Stunned, I looked back the way I had come. It was still early. Only a few people were up and about, their vague shadow shapes moving through the pervading greyness. Darker shapes of motor vehicles whispered silently by. It was too early for the morning rush. Overhead a solitary grey gull wheeled, curiously mute.

Not a sound reached me. Either I was deaf or I had been completely cut off from the 'outside' world. I had been badly shaken by my experience with Annette, and I *had* bolted through her front door. I sat down—not on the footpath but on the interface—and studied my predicament.

One: I now had no physical contact with the 'outside' world. I walked on an invisible membrane which I called the interface; it kept me isolated from everything that mattered.

Two: I now had only a tenuous visual contact with my previous world. There was a multitude of individual grey shapes; some were the ghostly reminders of human beings, some were buildings, still others were inanimate objects which I had to look at closely to identify. Outlines were blurred, features almost indistinguishable.

Three: I had lost all auditory contact with the 'outside' world.

Four: the interface that supported me was also a kind of prison.

Five—and this really shook me: It seemed possible that I could now move freely through what had once been solid objects in my previous world.

I tested this theory several times. I passed my hands cautiously through the stout trunk of a nearby tree; they met with no resistance. Growing bold, I deftly kicked my right foot through a fire hydrant; same result. The 'outside' world lacked substance. From my viewpoint it was a ghost universe, a dreadful parody of the world I remembered.

Walking was difficult at first. I had to get accustomed to the slippery interface. But I persevered, and although I slipped many times, I never fell. I assumed that the interface also kept me correctly aligned in this nightmare world.

I wandered morosely through the greyworld, feeling more lost than I imagined any human being had ever felt before.

Limbo.

I dredged the name from somewhere in my cluttered memory. I think it must have been a literary allusion, but I couldn't remember the source. The Bible? Perhaps. The idea brought to me a vision of a region of neglect, of abandonment. A place of oblivion or a haven for lost souls, for discarded and forgotten people. Something like that. I was very confused. Discarded and forgotten by *whom*? That was what bothered me most: the great unanswered question. And the greyness seemed deeper than before.

I somehow managed to keep moving along the interface. There was really nothing else I could do. I was afraid that if I stopped for more than a moment, I would never get up again. And while I walked I wondered about the vast, silent greyworld and people who disappeared without trace, missing persons whose absence left no logical explanation. I wondered how many of them had suffered my fate. Perhaps God was a clumsy bookkeeper.

I considered Bishop Berkeley's famous conundrum about the tree in the courtyard: Was it there when there was no one to look at it? And I asked myself: Had I ceased to exist in the outside world because people had ceased to notice me?

I thought of Omar Khayyam:

> *'Tis but a Chequer-board of Nights and Days*
> *Where Destiny with Men for Pieces plays;*
> *Hither and Thither Moves, and mates, and slays,*
> *And one by one back in the closet lays.*

Was I dead?

The possibility chilled me. I had no memory of an illness or of any impending demise. I recoiled violently from the implication. Then I grew angry, and I remembered reading somewhere that when you're faced with a difficult problem and you get angry, why then you can act—you can do something about it.

I could not and would not accept the theory that I had 'died' in the way that I understood the word. The events leading up to my 'displacement' did not support this idea—nor did the pounding pulse in my throat; it was all the proof I needed to convince me that I was still alive and that something strange had overtaken the world.

I was still afraid, but I was determined to do something. It was not enough to stroll around and bemoan my fate. I would discover the secret of my imprisonment or die in the attempt.

All around me the ghostly rush hour had begun. I saw the blurred shapes of cars hurtling by without making a sound. Trams clanged silently down the centre of the road. Pedestrians hurried on their way to work, some seeking buses and trams, others hastily hailing passing cabs. And all this but a pantomime played out in varying shades of grey. People passed by me and around me and *through* me. I discovered that I had no more substance in their world than they had in mine. The curiously muffled sound of my own feet stumbling along the interface was the only break in this absurd continuity.

Then from somewhere nearby I heard a dog bark.

THIS SUDDEN and unexpected sound transfixed me. The noise increased in vigour; it sounded like a small animal—a terrier, perhaps—lost and lonely and afraid, like myself.

Here, in Limbo?

Well, why not? I asked myself. It seemed possible that not only people but other life forms might get displaced from time to time. In which case—

I might not be alone after all. My heart raced at the possibility. But my sense of direction was unreliable. It had become disoriented by recent events. Try as I would, I could not trace the source of the sound—and it grew weaker every moment.

I made out the hazy outlines of a park on my left. Reason returned; I knew where I was. The barking brought forth no echo, but that was not surprising. It seemed likely that the animal would be somewhere in the park, so I hurried off quickly in that direction, slithering and sliding but somehow remaining upright on the slippery interface.

The soulful cry of the animal faded to a whimper. Poor creature! If we made contact then neither of us need feel alone. And if a dog had been displaced into my world then there was also the possibility that I might encounter other human beings . . .

But even as I ran through the park, blundering through the phantom shapes of bushes, trees, and benches, with no idea where the poor animal was, the air became suddenly still. As still as it had been before. Only my own hoarse breathing filled the greyworld. The barking was not repeated.

I stood quite still, straining my ears to pick up the slightest sound. I waited a long time, but I never heard that dog again.

Could I have imagined it?

No.

The sound had been real—as searing and as soulful as anything I had felt inside me since this mysterious business had begun. It had not been a renegade memory, but the first proof that I was not alone in this godforsaken place.

It was possible that I was not the first human being to have suffered the transition from the 'outside' world into Limbo—and certainly not the last. But if others had experienced this before me, why had they not returned to tell their stories?

I recoiled from the possible answer. Had it been because they had never returned?

I faced a forlorn hope—but without it I did not see how I could survive in this dreary place. And then there was a matter of food: without it I would starve. Now I could not eat anything from 'outside'—I would not even be able to grasp it; the interface would see to that. What then were my chances of discovering sustenance in Limbo?

I dragged my feet. They made a soft, soughing sound on the interface. I thrust my hands in my pockets again and looked downcast. Then I saw a splash of colour on the pavement.

I froze. The unexpected reappearance of colour in my monochromatic world dazzled me. Not that the object itself was unusually vivid: only a seagull, but the subtle shading of white and grey was a stunning contrast to the rest of my world. These colours *lived*.

I stooped down to investigate, my hands shaking with excitement. I could tell from its glazed eyes and lolling head that the bird was dead. I picked it up gently, feeling the last of its bodily warmth trickling through my fingers. Its yellow beak hung open and its sad eyes stared bleakly into death. There were no marks to indicate that it had been injured in any way.

Probably died of hunger.

And so might I.

A grim reminder of my position. I laid the bird gently on the edge of the side of the footpath—of the interface, that is—and straightened up, rubbing my hands on my jacket.

First the barking of an unseen dog, now a dead seagull. Limbo might not be as deserted as I had supposed, but the pathetic bundle at my feet was a warning of how my own fate might turn out if I did not find some source of food and drink. Already my mouth was parched with thirst.

I stepped around the dead seagull and resumed walking. This time I paid considerably more attention to my vague surroundings. I peered intently into the many shapes of the greyworld, searching for further signs of life or colour. I even discovered that once I allowed myself to relax, the silence was not as absolute as I had first thought. My irrational panic had brought on a psychic storm of such proportions that the subtle breath of Limbo had been drowned.

I began picking up isolated scraps of sounds, none of which made any sense. Combined they formed a constant background murmur that moved like a languid breeze through the greyworld, skating along the periphery of audibility.

I felt that the very air I breathed was charged with a curious potential, as though every particle, every atom, were busy maintaining an extraordinary tension.

But how much of this existed inside my own head

and how much was part of the ambience of the greyworld I could not be sure. I determined not to probe my own motives too deeply and to follow what proof I could find. I was confident it would only be a matter of time before—

Time. That was the big problem. I could not waste a moment. I would have to press on through the enveloping greyness until I found nourishment. And I was spurred on in my quest by the newfound knowledge that—

I was *not* alone.

I was not *alone.*

I was not alone.

I kept repeating this refrain over and over to myself. It helped to sustain my sudden burst of activity. The beauty and patience of Annette still haunted me, but I cast her angrily out of my thoughts. I could not count on the past—at least not until I had solved the riddle of the greyworld and my presence in it. And this I was determined to do—if there was enough time.

I passed briefly through a shopping centre. Farther on I moved into an older, residential area. I was surrounded by towering brick walls that ensured privacy, but I occasionally glimpsed luxuriant grey gardens where retired people lived out the last years of their lives in reasonable splendour.

I stopped suddenly. Another spot of colour had caught my attention. And this time it was no simple blend of grey and white but the vivid red of a small rose!

I was through the gate in a flash, flailing and stumbling my way across the interface until I reached that impossible flower. I was almost blinded by its unexpected brilliance, so accustomed had my eyes become to the greyworld. Then I very carefully snapped the rose free from the stem. Some flecks of blood appeared on my fingers to show where real thorns had pierced my skin. I did not care. It was a luxury to be reminded that I was alive—and human.

I looked down in wonder at the tiny rose. Why such a flower—here? I wondered. But then, why a dead bird and a barking dog I had not seen? Nothing made sense in the greyworld. If there was any pattern in Limbo it had so far eluded me.

I placed the rose carefully in my left jacket pocket and continued on my way, deep in thought.

I couldn't eat flowers. But if I had found a displaced rose then surely there was a chance I would discover something edible—anything that would keep me alive?

With this thought in mind I turned around and made a determined assault on the main shopping areas of St Kilda. I searched the 'outside' supermarkets and delicatessens and after an hour or so my ambition was rewarded. In one store the brilliant flash of a fresh orange stood out boldly among the grey mounds it was supposed to be part of. I grabbed it hungrily. It had also been ... displaced.

I fell upon the fruit greedily and devoured it with relish and without the slightest feeling of guilt. It tasted beautiful. Later on I found a packet of dried fruit and some nuts—even a small loaf of rye bread, several days old. My spirits soared. I began to walk with a swagger. The tricky interface of Limbo no longer worried me. I had found my legs at last.

I was convinced that I would not starve—at least not for some time. But I would be careful and conserve what I found. When I consulted my wristwatch and saw to my surprise that it was nearly four in the afternoon, I realised just how much of my time would be spent simply looking for food in this accursed place. The prospect

My eyelids drooped, my head slumped forward. Exhaustion hit me like a wave, but for a while sleep remained elusive. Pale faces rose before me. Annette's first —her serious questioning expression, her small mouth, a dark curl falling across one eye. Annette laughing. Annette arguing. Annette loving. Annette—

—a ghost now. Like everyone else.

I felt a knife twist in my chest.

I saw my parents dining quietly together at a table set for two.

The inscrutable face of Dr Birch.

The parade of ghostly faces continued until they merged into a whirling, confused vortex. My mind protested this invasion.

'Help me!' I cried out.

But who could hear me now?

Eventually I did fall into a fitful sleep. I felt no need of blankets; the temperature remained curiously constant in the greyworld. My last conscious thought was of the small body of the dead seagull which I had held fleetingly in my hands, and the warmth of its life trickling away through my fingers . . .

I WAS awakened next morning by the sound of someone playing a flute.

That was my first impression. But as I became more alert I recognised the more archaic timbre of a recorder.

I sat up with a start, forgetting for a moment where I was. Then I saw the greyworld of the hotel and I knew that it had not been merely a bad dream: I really was in Limbo. But the sound of someone playing an instrument astonished me—it was so unexpected.

I knew the melody. It was 'Greensleeves.' The most languid and melancholy of all English folk songs. It was being played with skill and considerable feeling, by someone who knew perfectly the limitations and also the very special qualities of the simple instrument, and I remember thinking that it suited the greyworld very well indeed.

But—a musician, here, in Limbo? The idea seemed absurd. Yet the sound persisted, fetching me awake.

It was a few minutes after eight. I had slept long and deeply. A few shadow shapes moved around 'outside' as the motel slowly accelerated to meet the new pulse of the day.

I stood up, wavering for a moment before I found my balance on the interface. The haunting melody sounded close. It seemed to come from somewhere outside near the entrance to the hotel.

I hurried outside, eager to meet another human being. But I found the grey street deserted. Only the silent trams and motor vehicles slid down the wide road. I peered into the distance as far as I could, but no figure did I see. Closing my eyes, I let my ears concentrate on the sound, and through them gained some sense of direction.

The player had moved off to my right, in the direction of the Junction. I hurried after him, following the melody that rose and fell at the whim of the unseen player.

The sound wandered, this way and then that through the interminable greyworld. I followed it down a narrow side street and into Queens Road. On the other side of the golf links the ugly grey surface of Albert Park Lake was sprawled motionless like an enormous sheet of hammered aluminium.

The melody pulled me along, but still I saw no human figure. Surely, I asked myself, a sound could not exist by itself in this continuum? But then, if objects—animate or otherwise—could be displaced, then why not—?

I pinned my hopes on a human player, not a fugitive tune. Sometimes the sound grew feeble; often I could not hear it at all. It was as though the player paused for a moment, perhaps considering his own predicament. Then the haunting melody would resume, and I would follow, trusting my ears when I could no longer trust my eyes.

The tune moved steadily ahead, turned right, and crossed a busy intersection filled now with the silent flow of early-morning traffic. I crossed Fitzroy Street and followed the elusive sound up Princes Street, feeling the interface begin to angle steeply where it followed the rising contour of the hill. *Clever.* Then ahead of me I saw—

A man wearing a long brown overcoat grown threadbare with age. He had on one of those funny French berets and a long woollen scarf wrapped around his neck; it was made up of bright yellow and orange stripes and it fell halfway down his broad back. His boots were shabby, the cuffs of his trousers ragged. He walked slowly, piping his melancholy tune. He did not seem to be aware that I was following him.

The sight of this stranger took my breath away. He loomed as solid and as real as myself. The magnificent striped colours of his long scarf were the most beautiful thing I had seen since I had been displaced. I was not alone anymore!

I felt an urge to rush forward and grasp the stranger's shoulder before he disappeared, just to make sure that he was real. But a more cautious side of my nature suggested I should hold back, bide my time, wait and see. After all, I had no way of knowing what manner of man I had chanced upon . . .

He stopped suddenly. The melody died. I stood quite still, wondering what would happen next. We were separated by a distance of several paces.

He turned around and studied me. I got the impression that he had been aware of my presence for some time, had known I was following him, and that he, too, had 'bided his time' before this confrontation.

He was old. A face deeply etched not only with the passage of time but with the burden of years. He looked like one who had suffered much. I placed his age between fifty and sixty; it was difficult to tell. He had about six weeks' growth of beard and his eyes were a watery hazel; they looked kind enough—but they marked me shrewdly.

We stared at each other for a long moment. My heart raced. I didn't know what to think. The stranger regarded me with narrow eyes. I returned his gaze with what I hoped was a frankly curious stare.

Suddenly his bearded face spread into a broad grin. He threw wide his arms in an expansive gesture of welcome and said in a voice heavy with brogue, 'Well, what have we here, now—another waif?'

I felt the blood rush to my cheeks. Alone and helpless I might well be, but a waif was a homeless, lost child. And I was a man.

'Somethin' new cast into this world and discarded from another, eh? And without so much as a by-your-leave?' His expression grew grave. He beckoned me.

But I stood my ground. I was not ready to commit myself. 'My name is Graeme Drury,' I said in a voice that wavered nervously. It had been so long since I had spoken to anyone but myself! 'I am seventeen years old and I am *not* a child.'

'Aye, that I can see, sure enough. But I meant no offence, Graeme. We're all waifs here, if it comes to that. Got nothin' to do with age. I'm Jamie Burns. You may call me Jamie, if you wish.' And he held out his hand—the right one; his left grasped the recorder.

I hesitated, then stepped forward and grasped the offered hand firmly. His grip was equally strong. There was warmth in his smile and I soon felt at ease. I was sure now that I had found a friend . . . and an ally.

'You said there were . . . others?'

He did not answer straight away. Instead he inclined his head to one side and studied me with his keen eyes. 'You been followin' me for some time, young fellow. Well, if you care to come a little further, I'll interduce you to a friend of mine. Mind you, I'm not pressin', lad. If you'd rather go about your own business . . .'

I thought there was a spark of mischief in the way he spoke, and I wondered what kind of a companion I had discovered who found time for humour in the greyworld. I must have looked confused, because he leaned forward and rested a gentle hand upon my shoulder and said softly, 'How long have you been here?'

I had to think hard to remember. So much had happened to me since I had been . . . displaced. 'About . . . two days, I think. I'm not sure. Everything . . . blurs. It's hard to—'

'I know.' He nodded his head sagaciously. 'Time moves differently here.'

'Does it?' I consulted my wristwatch. 'How do you know?'

'You begin to feel it, after a while.' He tapped my watch with a finger. 'Don' pay too much attention to that. It still keeps "outside" time. All mechanical things do. Sleep when you're tired, eat when you're hungry— and follow your own nose. That way you won' go wrong.'

'How do you know?'

He shrugged. 'It jus' works, that's all.'

I said, 'Do you find very much? I mean food and

things like that?'

He shook his head. 'A little.'

I told him quickly about the dead bird I had seen, the dog I had heard barking, and the food I had scrounged. I made no mention of the fabulous rose I still kept in my pocket; I would keep that for another time. At the moment it seemed inappropriate.

'There was a long while,' I explained, 'before I . . . was displaced. When things were kind of . . . mixed up.' And I told him some of my terrifying experiences.

'You've had a bad time, all right,' he said. 'A right rough 'un. But now you'll do best if you take things easy. Come on, I'll show you our place . . .'

There was something about him—an air of quiet dignity—that contrasted strongly with his run-down appearance. I decided to trust him. I was thankful to have discovered another human being to share my loneliness. And he *had* mentioned others . . .

As I followed him up the rising slope of the interface I saw a solid, two-story house standing out from the greyworld. It seemed a miracle: the sight of a brick building set apart from its shadowy companions gave me quite a shock. And it *was* real—as real as the old man and myself.

As we drew closer I could see that it had once been a fine mansion. It was now in an advanced state of decay —the kind of building that would quickly be condemned in the 'outside' world. The wrought-iron fence in front had collapsed like a wilted vine. The small garden was a forest of strangling weeds. Wide cracks had sundered the faded pink cement rendering of the facade; huge chunks of it had fallen away in many places, exposing the ancient red bricks underneath. Bright new curtains covered one of the ground-floor windows facing the street; a ragged old blanket was drawn across the other. The upper two were bare, staring back at me like vacant eyes. An emaciated gathering of ivy was struggling to maintain a precarious hold upon this once-stately home, but it was slowly withering away.

Ancient and decayed it might be, but this was the first real house I had seen in Limbo. The old man who called himself Jamie Burns motioned me toward it. 'Come on, lad . . .'

I followed him over the fallen fence and through the tangled garden of weeds.

'Bet you didn' expect to see anythin' like a house again, eh?' he said. 'Well, some mighty strange things come through. You've seen some of them yourself. Saw a truck, yesterday. All kinds of rubbish. Not much of it useful, though . . .'

He pushed open the front door. It had not been locked. He smiled. 'Nothin' to be afraid of, lad. There's only myself and one other lives here. Not that you could call it livin', mind you . . .'

I followed him inside. A long, narrow hallway stretched out ahead. The walls were covered with a network of cracks, and bits of plaster littered the faded carpet. Some old paintings and photographs hung askew on the walls and the carpet *stank*: a musty, acrid smell that reminded me of some of the old apartments I had played in as a child.

The old man shrugged. 'It's home, Graeme. The only one we have . . .' He motioned toward the open door on our right. 'In there is what we jokin'ly call our livin' room . . .'

It was almost as run-down as the hallway—but not quite. The walls were as cracked, and long strips of faded wallpaper had peeled away in places and curled up on the carpet. Newspapers and magazines and paperback books were scattered across the floor. There was a wooden table set against the window and two kitchen chairs. I saw a large black bean bag chair in one corner and the remains of many meals scattered amid the debris of cans and packets piled high on the table. The air smelled slightly better than that in the hallway. There was an old open fireplace on my left.

A small fire burned in the tiny grate. Before it sat a young woman wearing faded brown cords and a beige sweater. She had her legs crossed and she looked up, like a startled cat, when we came in. Her eyes were cold and hard as they studied me. I felt a wave of hostility reach out and catch me off guard. I did not know what to say.

The old man stepped forward. 'Marion, found me another. Only recently come through. His name's Graeme . . .'

She did not relax her scrutiny. I had an impression of cool, green eyes and an intelligent face; long straggly blond hair that fell past her shoulders. She was slender (like Annette), with small breasts and tiny ankles. Her skin was pale. Her feet were bare. She regarded me dispassionately.

'Graeme,' Jamie said quietly, 'this is Marion . . .'

I nodded. I felt like a specimen pinned by her steady look. Then she allowed herself to relax. Her hostily vanished. 'Hello, Graeme,' she said softly. But her voice was as cold as her green eyes. She was not beautiful, but her manner affected me in an extraordinary way. Perhaps this was a result of the heightened state of existence we all led at that moment.

'Come here,' she said. 'Sit down. It's warm by the fire. Sorry we haven't got much in the way of furniture. We only get what comes through, and what Jamie retrieves.' She looked back at the fire and sat with her head hunched forward in her hands.

I sat down beside her. Jamie went over to the table

and emptied the capacious pockets of his overcoat. It reminded me of one of Harpo Marx's old routines—the bottomless pockets and so forth. I could not restrain a smile. It had been a long while since I had been amused by anything.

'Not *too* bad,' the old man announced proudly. 'Two cans of sweet corn—'

'Argh,' said Marion.

'—a bread roll, a can of tomatoes, a small packet of spaghetti, and—' He made a flourish and held aloft of a small, dark bottle. 'Drambuie! What do you think of that for luck, lass?'

He was obviously delighted with his prize. I could almost feel his tongue sliding over his lips in anticipation. But Marion gave him a sharp look. 'Is that all?' she snapped. 'No milk? Not even a can of soft drink?'

His face fell. 'Sorry, lass. I really tried hard. Looked everywhere. Couldn' find anythin' else—'

'Bloody hell,' Marion muttered, and glanced at the fire.

'I'll go out again in the afternoon,' Jamie hastened to add. Then his manner changed and for a moment he looked a little aggressive. 'That's unless *you* feel like it. Have you been out yet?'

She gave a contemptuous flick of her blond hair. 'No, I haven't. Not yet. Canned corn and whisky. Shit.' She stared moodily into the fire. I felt she was deliberately ignoring my presence while she concentrated her hostility on the old man.

I found the strain of their relationship unsettling. 'Please,' I said, emptying my little plastic bag of my provisions, 'where on Earth are we? I've been wandering around in this greyworld for so long trying to figure out what happened to me, why I'm here. And I haven't any answers. You . . . you people—you've been here longer.

Surely you must have some idea?'

The old man shook his head. For a moment his confrontation with the girl was put aside. 'Sorry to disappoint you, lad. Sad fact of the matter is that neither of us has any more idea than yourself. Let's see—I've been here for, oh, going on to four weeks, I suppose. The way I reckon time, and believe you me, it isn' all that easy. Marion has been here for two. But as to how we came to be here . . .' He shrugged. 'No idea at all . . .'

My hopes dwindled. I had been expecting some form of explanation, however tenuous. Something to go on.

Marion said, 'All Jamie has is theories.' She sounded bitter.

'Aye, that I have.' The old man sat down at the table, placed his recorder carefully in his coat pocket. He clasped his hands and looked at me. 'Why not? A man has to occupy his mind in some way. I'm not one for sittin' around all day feelin' sorry for myself.' I felt this was a barbed criticism of his companion. Marion did not rise to the bait. 'But then, haven' you figured some of it out for yourself, lad?'

I shook my head.

'Why, we're the forgotten ones, Graeme!'

Forgotten? 'I don't quite see your point.'

Jamie eyed me shrewdly. 'Would you by any chance be a Christian? Not one of the church-goin' variety, you understand. The real thing.'

I thought about that for a moment. Religion was something I had given a lot of thought over the past few years. It was a task I had approached without ever expecting a resolution, just discovering a code of conduct. 'I . . . I'm not sure,' I answered. Truthfully. 'At least, not yet. And I don't go to church, either. I have studied comparative religions—'

'A wise move.'

'—and the existentialists interest me. But for the moment—'

'Haven' made up your mind, or drawn any conclusions. As they say.' The old man gave a deep sigh and settled back in his chair. 'Can' say as I blame you. It's a cockeyed world, all right. Youngsters of today must find it heavy going. Too many contradictions, political and otherwise. Too many choices—and God losing out all along the line. Well, that's His worry. He should have organised things more in His favour. Now, in my day it was easier—things were either black or white. God and king and country. Simple. Why, I even worshipped Winston Churchill. Can you imagine that?' He leaned forward. 'Dabbled in religion, have you? Then I suppose you've worked your way through Nietzsche as well?'

'A little.'

'Yeah—tough old bastard. Heavy-goin' Teutonic. Germans are like that. Serious.'

'Yes.' *What was he leading up to?*

'Zarathustra and all that.' He made a deprecating noise. 'I only mention him in passin'. You see, if you accept the possibility of a Supreme Bein'—God or Whateve; call it a force, if you prefer, it makes more sense—then you also have to accept that there is a Divine Order in the universe. If there is a God, then it could be that He is not dead—as Nietzsche would have us believe—but a little . . . absentminded, perhaps? His eye may very well be on the sparrow, but I think He occasionally forgets other aspects of His realm. People, for example. Looking after Creation must keep Him busy, so I suppose it's only to be expected that He slips from time to time . . .'

'Oh, Jamie,' Marion snapped, exasperated. 'You do carry on! Can't you see the boy's frightened out of his wits? Do you think that feeding him your metaphysical rubbish is going to make him feel any better?'

I appreciated her speaking up for me, for in truth I found the old man's wild ideas difficult to swallow—but I took exception to the tone in her voice when she used the word 'boy.' She was possibly a year older than I—no more. Did I look so lost and helpless in her eyes that she thought of me . . . as a child?

'The lad was only seeking answers,' Jamie said defensively.

'Crap.' Marion looked away—gave me a fleeting smile of reassurance for which I was grateful—and stared again into the fire. 'You're full of it, Jamie. Day in, day out—it's all I hear. It wouldn't be so bad if you weren't so damned dogmatic. I don't see how it matters if God is dead or if He just does not wish to get involved. Nothing here makes sense and you're wasting our time trying to work it out. We might just as well be midges trying to unravel the mysteries of the universe, or goldfish staring out of a bowl. If you want to hear *my* opinion—for what it's worth—then I think we're forgotten because people out there'—she waved one hand expansively to take in the greyworld—'people *out there* have just forgotten us. Not God, not a Supreme Being or force—just people like ourselves. We don't matter anymore.'

I gave her a curious look. 'Do you really believe that?'

She shrugged. 'It's no crazier than some of Jamie's theories. You should hear him when he gets going on the Cosmic Filing Clerk—'

'Now, wait a moment,' the old man interjected. 'I've never looked at it that way before. You could be onto something. Perhaps we only exist in relationship to someone else's concept of ourselves, and vice versa.' He paused, perhaps only too aware of the deep philosophical waters he was wading into. He sighed. 'Well, be that as it may, we are stuck here. And here we seem destined to stay.'

'Until we starve,' Marion pointed out, eyes narrowed.

Jamie shook his head. 'No, lass. There'll be no starvin' here, not while I have anything' to do with it. We'll endure. Trust me. And we have Graeme to help us now—'

'And one more mouth to feed.' She gave me an apologetic smile, but soon grew serious again. 'What do we do when the food runs out? There's a limit to how far we can walk every day . . .'

I couldn't stand this senseless bickering any longer. I stood up. 'Look, do you have to keep sniping at each other? I've been through hell. We've *all* been through hell—'

'Then is this purgatory?' Marion snapped.

'Quiet, lass,' Jamie hissed.

'—so for God's sake let's stop bickering and try and act like rational human beings.'

'Easily said,' Marion said. She sounded sullen. 'See how you feel after you've been stuck here for a few weeks . . .'

'The lad's right,' Jamie said forcefully. Then his voice softened. 'Don' pay too much attention to us, Graeme. She's a strong-willed one, sure enough—but a good worker, when she sets her mind to it.' Marion's jaw formed a hard line and she did not smile. 'Come over here and sit down,' the old man went on, motioning me to the spare chair. 'Are you hungry? You look hungry. Try a piece of Polish sausage; it's not too bad. And there's a bit of cheese left over, and that rye bread you just brought in. It's a few days old, but that doesn' matter. Better than your sliced white plasticine, eh?' He laughed at his joke and made an orderly arrangement of these items for me as I sat down. 'I think there's a drop of milk left in the carton— No, sorry. It's gone.'

'I drank it,' Marion said. 'I was thirsty.' She sat with

her back to us. Jamie winked slyly and nodded in her direction, trying to reassure me that this most unsociable young woman was not as bad as she seemed. They were an odd couple, all right, And I suppose we made an equally strange trio . . .

Jamie handed me his small pocketknife—one of those Swiss Army types that have everything that opens and shuts—and I hacked off a long piece of the dried sausage. It was only when I began eating that I realised how hungry I was.

Jamie watched me. 'We have to make do with what we find,' he apologised. I was in no mood to complain. I chewed away thoughtfully, wondering about the old man and the girl, what their lives had been before, like me, they had been cast into the greyworld.

'Jamie,' I said after a while, 'what did you do . . . before?'

A misty, melancholy expression settled over his tired face. He took out his recorder and began toying with it, a faraway look in his eyes. 'Do? I've done many things in my time, young fellow—though sometimes it's hard to remember them all. Where would you like me to begin?'

'Anywhere.' He had the look of someone who had been around a lot and seen many changes. I hadn't done much at all—except go to school. I seemed to have been at school all my life . . .

He said, 'You'll be goin' to university, I suppose?'

'Was,' I corrected. I saw no point now in contemplating a future that might never be. 'Or rather, I hoped to. There were a lot of things up in the air—'

'I used to go to university—in Queensland. That was a long time ago.'

'What did you do there?'

'Oh, the usual. Mucked about for the most part.

Doesn' everybody? I eventually did settle down to serious study. I taught . . . music.' He waved the recorder at me. 'Not just this, mind you. Theory and all. The oboe was my first instrument, and truly marvellous it is! Cello was second. But that was long ago and many lifetimes away.'

'Many lifetimes?'

'Figure of speech. I, ah, also majored in philosophy.'

From the direction of the fireplace I distinctly heard a deprecating laugh.

Jamie said, 'You must forgive the lady's rudeness, Graeme. We don' always see eye to eye on some matters, as you have already deduced. But until you happened along we had only each other. Can' say as her upbringin' "outside" has been very beneficial—'

'I didn't choose my present company,' the girl snapped irritably.

'Aye, that's true enough. But we have to make the best of what we have, like the boy said.' The old man's voice dropped to a near whisper when he explained how he had found her, wandering in the greyworld and crying hysterically. Lost, lonely, and afraid, and with no shoes on her feet and a wild look in her eyes like a frightened deer.

I digested this information slowly. The girl made no movement, nor did she make any comment. I grew curious and emboldened enough to ask how each of them had 'come through,' as Jamie called it.

The old man said, 'Well, I fell asleep on the beach one afternoon—'

'You were drunk,' Marion said quietly, but the edge of hostility was absent from her words.

'Well, now, come to think of it I might have had a little drink, but I wouldn' say that I was, well, fallin'-down drunk.'

'Drunk,' she repeated. But her manner had softened and I sensed she was baiting him more gently than before. I could not see her face but I was sure that a soft smile played around her lips.

'Yes. Well, we won' go any further into that. Like I was explainin', I fell asleep. The sun was warm; the sand was comfortable; there was a nice breeze comin' in from the sea. It was a Thursday, as I recall. Not many people around. Anyway, when I woke—it must have been in the middle of the afternoon—I discovered that everythin' nearby was drained of colour. At first I thought a fog had rolled in from the sea, and when that seemed wrong I wondered if my eyesight was playing up. When there were no sounds as well I began to get worried. The lack of any sound at all—that was the worst part.'

'It happened so quickly?' I could hardly believe it. 'Could you . . . touch anything? Was there anything you could grasp or pick up?'

He shook his head. 'That was the worst part. I couldn' touch a thing. And when I stood up there was only an odd, slippery surface underfoot—something I couldn' see. And still can't. But I'm used to it now. We both are.'

'The interface,' I said soberly.

'Eh?'

I explained my theory of the invisible membrane that apparently separated us from the 'outside' world. Jamie nodded thoughtfully. The idea obviously intrigued him. Even Marion turned around from the fire and studied me with a new respect.

'It was different for me,' I went on, and told them of the bewildering train of events that had led up to my final displacement into the greyworld.

'Christ,' Marion exclaimed, 'that must have been awful for you!'

'I can assure you it was.' Her concern pleased me. It enabled me to relax and feel more 'at home.'

'And how about you?' I asked carefully. 'Did you have a bad time . . . coming through?'

Her features became suddenly devoid of expression, like a plaster mask. 'Bad enough,' she replied. And would not elaborate.

'Marion doesn' talk much about it,' Jamie hastened to explain. 'At least, not to me. Maybe she'll open up a bit more when she gets to know you.'

The girl said nothing. Instead she turned around and resumed her vigil by the fire. I thought of my family, my friends, my hopes and ambitions. Gone now. And for the first time understood the old man's melancholy manner and the girl's grim countenance. I said to Jamie, 'Did you leave anyone behind?'

My question evoked in him a peculiar depression. He fondled the recorder absently, his eyes roved nervously around the decrepit room. 'Not really,' he said. 'There was someone—long ago. A woman. A . . . great lady. But I think I was much too selfish to let myself get close enough to anyone to experience true love. I'm no great loss to the world, lad. But you—you must have left a family behind? A girlfriend, perhaps? Many acquaintances, certainly . . .'

Words eluded me; I could only nod. Already my past life had taken on the substance of a dream; it sometimes seemed like an elaborate fiction I had fashioned for my own amusement. Now only the moment mattered, and my friendship with these strangers.

I turned my attention to the girl, determined to try again. 'And how about you, Marion?'

'Nothing,' she replied. Her voice quite firm. 'I left nothing behind. Nothing that mattered.' She would not elaborate and, under the circumstances, I considered it prudent to let the matter lie. Perhaps at some later date, when we were better acquainted . . . ?

'God,' she muttered, breaking a long silence, 'what I wouldn't give for a cup of hot coffee!'

I was puzzled. 'But you have a small fire. I can see a jar of instant coffee on the table—'

She tossed her head. 'Oh, we've got fire all right— Jamie's very good at foraging for bits of wood, aren't you Jamie? And we do have some coffee left. What we don't have is *water*.' She gave me a hard look. 'Have you ever tried washing yourself with soft drink? No? Well, you may jolly well have to.'

The prospect was unappealing. 'You can make coffee with milk,' I suggested.

'Doesn't taste the same.'

Jamie rolled his eyes heavenward in a gesture of impatience.

I said, 'Well, can we really afford to be so fussy?'

'Marion can,' the old man interjected. He spread his hands in a weary gesture of resignation.

I had a bright idea. 'Have you checked out the supermarkets for bottled mineral water? That would do.' They both looked at me blankly. 'But surely some of it must have come through, along with all the other stuff?'

Marion was looking respectfully at me again. 'Mineral water,' she echoed. 'Now why didn't I think of that?'

'If the bubbles bother you,' I hurried on, 'they'll boil out. Or leave the bottles open until the water goes flat.'

Jamie said, 'First we have to find some. I'm not sure it will be all that easy. Only a little of everything comes through . . .'

'But it's worth trying!' I felt desperate now, and determined to do what I could to brighten up our miserable exile.

The old man sighed again, more deeply than before. 'Well, we can give it a try. What do you think, Marion? You're the one who hankers after coffee.'

The girl nodded her blond head thoughtfully. 'It's possible. We've found other bottled drink—why not mineral water? Graeme's right. It's worth a try.'

Now Jamie said carefully, 'Then why don' you show the lad around the local supermarkets and such? Help him get started. Orientated and all that. You might find somethin' else that might be useful while you're at it. I'll look after the fire . . .'

She hesitated. 'There isn't much wood left,' she said defensively. Obviously she resented being told what to do. Despite their wrangling I thought that the old man treated her kindly enough. I formed the impression that her hostility toward any sort of authority went back a long way—before the greyworld. The trait seemed too deeply ingrained in her personality to have been recently acquired.

'I'll nurse along the little that's left,' Jamie said patiently. 'It will last a few hours. When you come back I'll go out again and see if I can find some more. And it would pay you both to keep your eyes sharp as well. Now, what do you say? Shall I show the lad around, or will you?'

Her green eyes appraised me with a touch of uncertainty. I waited nervously.

'Oh, all right, then,' she agreed. '*I'll* show him . . .'

She stood up and I saw that she was as tall as I and maybe a year older; it was hard to guess her age. She had the kind of face that encourages people to remark that the person in question has either been 'born old' or 'seen a lot of life'. I've never been quite sure what the terms mean, but I've taken them to describe people who always seem to be a little bit ahead of their contemporaries. She was a strange one, all right.

'Come on,' she said, stretching, 'let's get moving. We'll have a quick look around the food spots and see what we can find. You know this part of the city?'

I explained that I had lived in St Kilda for the past three years. This seemed to impress her. 'That will come in handy.' She spoke slowly and precisely and without any emotion whatsoever—except when her anger or petulance were directed at Jamie.

She noticed me staring at her bare feet. 'Shoes don't matter,' she said. 'Not here. It makes walking easier.'

'Now don't you two get lost,' the old man cautioned us. 'The greyness can fool you if you're not careful . . .'

Marion didn't even bother to reply. Without a backward glance she left the room, expecting me to follow. I hesitated for a moment, looked at Jamie. He shrugged, then gave me a warm smile and motioned for me to get going. So I did.

SHE MOVED quickly, her bare feet hardly seeming to touch the interface. She was more experienced at this sort of thing than I; I had to hurry to catch up to her.

'We'll try Safeway first,' she said. 'They're closest.' She looked straight ahead as we moved down the dull grey canyon I remembered as Barkly Street.

'That's a long walk,' I commented. All the way down to Carlisle Street and up to the Balaclava shopping centre.

'You get used to it.'

'Did you live around here too?' I asked, struggling to keep up with her.

'No. Up country. I was . . . visiting down here when it happened.' She stopped suddenly and looked at me. 'Can you tell me where the beach is from here?'

'Down there, to the right.'

She smiled. 'Full marks. I don't think you'll get lost. Jamie does worry a little too much, sometimes.'

I said, 'He cares. He doesn't seem such a bad old chap.'

She made no comment. We resumed our progress. She remarked that if we were out of luck at Safeway—the largest supermarket in the area—then we would have to make what she called the 'grand tour' of all the smaller places.

'Do you do this every day?' I asked.

'Have to. Jamie and me both. Except when I get lazy and feel like giving up.' A sparkle of mischief showed in her eyes. 'That's when we fight a bit. Jamie *never* gives up: day after day after day. We're scavengers, you see. Like the birds and animals "outside." Nearly all our time is taken up trying to locate enough food to keep alive.'

'But you always manage to find enough?'

She made a wry face. 'Not always. And canned corn isn't the most appetising of meals—at least not to me. But we outcasts have to be thankful for anything we can lay our hands on. We find more useless junk than edible food . . .'

I asked her what she meant by 'junk.'

'Mostly electronic garbage. Toasters, transistor radios, electric razors—that sort of thing. No use to us here. No power. Only batteries, when we can find them. But even old Jamie turned up his nose at a cordless shaver.' She laughed. It was a light, gentle sound, filled with warmth.

A vague possibility troubled me. 'Are there . . . any others—besides ourselves?'

'Not that I know of. Jamie says there used to be another man, but went kinda crazy after a while and wandered off into the greyness. Never saw him again. I've seen birds, now and then, flapping through the air. Not many, though. And sometimes I hear cats howling . . .'

I told her about the dead seagull. The story seemed to depress her. I made no mention of the precious rose in my pocket; I felt that our relationship was not well formed enough for me to exhibit such a treasure. Later, perhaps, she would understand and share my wonder.

I must have looked rather glum, for all of a sudden she stopped and tugged at my left sleeve. It was the first time we had touched, and despite the tentative nature of the gesture, it was the beginning of a bond between us. In this godforsaken world simple overtures of friendship carried an enormous weight.

'Look, Graeme,' she said, in a surprisingly gentle tone I hadn't heard her use before, 'don't give in to this thing. You just can't afford to let it get you down. I know. So does Jamie. There are only two things that we need to consider: *Why* are we here and *what* do we do about it? I haven't time to ponder over Jamie's wild theories; for me it's enough work just keeping alive. That's what we must concentrate all our efforts on, now that there are three of us. Does that make sense?'

I nodded. 'You're right. I . . . I didn't mean to look so doleful. It's just that sometimes—'

'I know. The past and all that.' She took my hand, folding her fingers gently in mine so that I would not mistake the gesture. 'But come on, now. Let's have a look in Safeway . . .'

A great burden seemed to rise from my shoulders when her hand nestled in mine, and for the first time since I had been thrust into the greyworld I felt hopeful that everything might eventually turn out for the better.

When we found the supermarket we walked through— again, literally *through*—the checkout area and stood surveying the long grey isles packed high with foodstuffs. Marion warned me that although the shelves were crammed with the blurry outlines of packages in the 'outside' world, they were also deep and could hide a genuine item of use. 'Real things that have come through are hard to find. You have to angle your head this way and that, look in every nook and cranny in order to find something. It's the only way. So take your time. We'll try this aisle first. The soft-drink department is at the far end . . .'

I let her move on ahead. She was more experienced than I at this sort of scavenging, and I was willing to watch and learn. I paid more attention to her hunting instinct than I gave to the ghostly shelves on either side of the aisle. She moved with the grace of a cat, a motion made up of half walking, half sliding along the interface, a technique she had perfected which allowed her bare feet to negotiate the tricky, invisible surface with surprising ease. My own movements were still a shambling, unsteady gait, with much waving about of hands to keep my balance. Marion's ease of movement astonished me; I hoped that in time I would be able to emulate it. She seemed perfectly at home on the interface, and this led me to wonder if perhaps this poise was a quality she had been born with, or had acquired later in life, and not learned through her displacement.

I turned my attention to the shadowy shelves. I recognised the blurred outlines of cereal packets, spaghetti, rice, and other dry foods. Without being aware of what I was doing—my attention had again been diverted to Marion—I walked *through* the ghostly figure of one of the supermarket staff, a young man kneeling with a clipboard resting on his knee, studiously taking an inventory of the bottom shelves. I felt queer all over. The 'ghost' gave no indication that he had felt my mysterious passage. Dazed, I wondered if I would ever get accustomed to the absurdities of the greyworld.

Marion had paused before the vast soft drink section at the far end of the aisle and was studying it wistfully. As I hurried to catch up with her I saw her lean forward and peer among the bottles. It was almost impossible to distinguish one label from another, but her practised eyes were not deceived.

'Well, there's mineral water, all right,' she said, '*and* soda water. But it's all "outside." Not even a can of Coke today. Blast. Oh, well, let's try somewhere else . . .'

She took her time leaving the supermarket; force of habit led her to check out each aisle in turn. 'Just in case,' she explained. 'You never know what might turn up . . .'

We were almost finished when she gave a sudden cry of delight and rushed forward. 'Look, Graeme! Over here . . .'

I saw a dazzling orange object lying on the 'floor.' As I drew closer it resolved into a folded blanket, one of many stacked 'outside.' Marion snatched it up with a shout of triumph. 'There. Isn't it beautiful?'

But it wasn't a blanket. It was an enormous orange beach towel. It was dazzling. She rubbed the fabric against her cheek and for a moment closed her eyes and sighed. I was very moved. Then she opened her eyes and gave me a fleeting smile. 'Here—you take it.' She held it out to me. 'It will make a good blanket.'

I hesitated. 'But the temperature seems steady . . .'

She shook her head. 'Not inside the house. That's the real world for us, remember? And it can get bloody cold.'

But I was firm. 'No, please keep it. It looks . . . good, when you hold it. The colours. They're dazzling.'

'Do you really think so? You're sure you don't mind?' She held the towel at arm's length, then wrapped it quickly around her, so that for a moment she looked like a mischievous tramp in a school play. 'It is lovely, isn't it? I've never found anything so beautiful before—what luck! Thanks, Graeme. If we can't find one for you, then you can have one of mine. I've got several back at the house. Okay?'

I said that would be all right. I felt embarrassed. She seemed so much at home in the drab greyworld while I had not even managed to grasp my predicament.

She stopped again near the checkout. She had discovered a miniature cassette recorder, one of the very latest models so popular with businessmen. She regarded it dubiously. It carried a red tag that screamed SPECIAL and a spare cassette taped to the back. It was real enough, but was it useful?

I said, 'Does it work?'

'I don't know. You try it.'

I did. The controls worked perfectly, so that meant the batteries were fresh. 'There's a tape inside,' I said. 'Looks like a long player . . .'

'I saw that. I was hoping that it might be prerecorded. We could do with a little music.'

I explained that this tiny machine was more of a business tool than a teenage toy. She was not impressed. 'There's a spare tape,' I told her, 'but it's blank.'

'Too bad.'

'We could make our own music,' I suggested. 'You must know a few songs, and I'm sure Jamie could be persuaded to help out with his recorder.'

She laughed. 'Oh, I know some *beauties,* all right.' Then she grew serious again, as though her mind had been jogged by an unpleasant memory. I was reminded again of the way she moved, with her chin slightly downcast as though she was not quite ready to face up to the world and its consequences, although she seemed quite at home in Limbo. And I did not think she had acquired this mannerism in the greyworld. Later conversations were to bear out my suspicion, but I did not pursue the subject now.

We concluded our 'haul' with a can of cream of oyster soup—to which Marion's only comment was 'Yuk!'—and then left the supermarket. She warned me to watch the sidewalk. 'Sometimes a cracked piece of cement sticks through from "outside" and you can catch your toe if you're not careful. Then there's occasional broken glass and bottles, the odd discarded beer can, a misplaced fire hydrant. That sort of thing.'

I took her advice. Again I let her move on a little ahead of me so that I could admire the graceful way she maneuvred across the interface. I did my best to follow her example, but it seemed it would take me some time before I could match her expertise.

We reached an intersection. I gazed longingly toward the beach, so close and yet so distant now in space and time. Marion guessed my mood correctly. 'Come on,' she said, grasping my free hand, 'there's something down there I want you to see . . .'

We crossed the busy intersection, myself bewildered by the hurtling great shapes of silence that were motor vehicles of every shape and size. Marion smiled and seemed to enjoy my confusion. 'You'll get used to it,' she said. 'After a while.' And I asked her why she seemed so at home in the greyworld.

'It's just another kind of prison,' she said, and would comment no further.

I did not so much run as get hauled along in her wake. Soon we were running downhill through the park —the palm trees towering overhead like indifferent giants, the interface adapting itself to the changing contours of the 'outside' world. I looked in vain for a splash of colour among the flowers, but found none.

We crossed the road that separated the park from the beach and Marion led me down onto the eerie grey sand. I remember her eyes were brighter than I had ever seen before and her pale cheeks bore a healthy flush.

We came to a stop, breathing heavily from our long run. I stared out to sea and this time I could see where it merged with the sky. It must have been a clear day 'outside' for the division to be so clear, yet I saw no sun in the sky and the greyworld was shrouded in its customary dusk.

Marion let go of my hand and pointed. 'Over there,' she said. 'Tell me what you see—quickly!'

But before I could respond she told me to take off my shoes. I did so and found it easier to cope with the slippery interface. 'Throw them away,' she said. 'You won't be needing them.' I saw no reason to argue, so I obliged. For a moment I could have sworn that my bare feet made contact with the sand in the 'outside' world, but I soon realised it was an illusion, a conditioned response: my feet had expected to feel the familiar scrunch of sand. The sensation soon passed, but the effect upon me lingered.

'Well,' Marion said impatiently, 'do you see anything unusual?' I followed the direction of her gaze. And only a few yards from where we stood a shallow rock pool protruded into *our* world.

I gave a gasp of surprise. Marion was pleased. 'Isn't it wonderful?' she exulted. I could only nod in reply. I was too dazed to say anything. It was all so unexpected...

I heard her happy laughter as I stumbled forward. I skidded to a stop when I realised that the interface had disappeared and that there was real sand under my feet. I sank to my knees, filled with wonder, and gazed at the pool. An arc of sand about a metre wide had also come through; it was warm and moist and gritty and very, very real. Part of the real world that was no longer real to me, displaced into Limbo with as little consideration as myself or a dead seagull. The pool was surrounded by a number of odd-shaped rocks encrusted with marine molluscs; it was about three metres across. I crawled forward and peered down into the water. The bottom of the pool bustled with minute life forms. I envied them their mindless ignorance of their condition.

I looked again out to sea, forgetting the can of soup I had been carrying and letting it fall onto the sand. I could see where a kind of veil had been drawn between the pool and the 'outside' water. I dipped the fingers of my right hand into the pool; I raised them to my lips and tasted the brine. I almost cried when a rush of memories washed over me.

Marion sat down carefully beside me. She looked calm and mysterious. We were so entranced by the miracle of the pool that neither of us spoke, for fear of shattering the priceless moment. But eventually she did —gently. 'I found it only yesterday,' she explained. 'Isn't it marvellous? A piece of the real world—I mean the *old* real world. Almost too good to be true, isn't it?'

I felt an extraordinary sensation. 'What time . . . yesterday?' I was trying to remember when I had left the beach the previous day.

She thought for a moment, brushing back her hair, which had been stirred by a rogue breeze. 'It was nearly dark. I had been out walking, all afternoon—looking for things. And . . . I like to walk along the beach at dusk, even here . . .'

I remembered my own reluctant retreat from the beach. There is something about the eternal nature of the sea that soothes the heart. It occurred to me that if I had stayed there a little while longer—

'I might have met you,' I said aloud.

She gave me a curious look. 'What do you mean?'

I told her. 'Why, we might have discovered the pool together!'

She looked quickly away. 'Perhaps we were not meant to.'

I thought that a strange thing to say, but I decided not to pursue the matter any further. The rock pool had taken command of my attention.

Marion handed me the vivid orange towel she had been carrying. 'Here, have a wash and dry yourself. It's better than washing in lemonade. Just your face and hands. It's not really deep enough for swimming . . .'

I needed no further encouragement. I cupped my hands and scooped up some of the salty water and dashed it in my face. It was so unexpectedly cold that it took my breath away. Marion laughed and urged me on. And so I did, splashing the ocean vigorously over my face and hands for several seconds until I tired of the game. I dried myself slowly with the orange towel, and when I was finished I looked down into the rock pool for a long time, brooding.

I was suspended in time and space. I watched the tiny fish—whitebait—darting around in the water, like trapped creatures searching for a way out of their prison. Their universe was not so vast as that of the teeming micro-organisms they shared the pool with, and like Marion and myself—and Jamie—they felt constrained and were driven by a blind instinct to escape back to the ocean from which they had been displaced. But their way back was barred; for like us they were doomed to remain in the greyworld forever. So ran the tenor of my thoughts.

'They're lost, Marion,' I said. 'Like us. They can't get

back . . .'

She leaned forward and I felt her hand upon my shoulder, sensed her face close to mine. 'I know. I've watched them, too . . . yesterday. But do you really think they matter? I mean, are they as important as us?'

I straightened up, struggling to contain my anger. 'If they are not, then the entire universe is a joke,' I said bitterly. And meant it.

She looked at me for a long moment, then let her gaze wander out across the grey sea. 'I have often wondered,' she said, 'if our world—the "outside" world as well as this—is only some kind of experiment. And if we are part of it, pawns in a game so vast that we cannot even begin to comprehend it, despite all our marvellous philosophers. Oh, I make fun of Jamie sometimes, but he's got a good head on his shoulders, you know. Maybe we are as uninformed as those tiny creatures in the pool —and always will be.'

I frowned. 'I thought you said you left all the metaphysics to the old man?'

A hurt expression flashed across her face. 'I'm sorry,' she said quickly. 'I . . . I didn't mean to upset you.'

'But you didn't . . .'

'Whatever happens,' she went on, 'we must try to be fair to each other, not hurt each other . . . Graeme. It's enough keeping up with Jamie's moods. Let's you and me just *do* things. That's why I brought you here—I knew you would appreciate the pool. Jamie . . . I don't think he'd care. Honest. I think he stopped caring about things long before he arrived here. Now all he worries about is finding enough booze to keep him going. And that bloody recorder of his!'

'Does he drink much?'

'He would—if he could find enough. And the only bloody tune he ever plays is that damned "Greensleeves"!'

'It's a lovely melody.'

'Tell me that in two weeks' time. You know, I think it must be connected with someone he knew "outside" —a long time ago.'

'That woman he mentioned?'

'Maybe. But he never talks about it.'

'Has he ever—'

'Bothered me? No. Never. When he found me I must have looked a sorry mess. He took me in and nursed me and taught me how not to be afraid. I'll always be thankful to him for that. "All the world's a dream, lass," he used to tell me, "and this no more than any other. We have to learn to live with what we have, and with each other." Yes, I think he must have lost all feeling for the "outside" world a long time ago. That's why he doesn't seem to miss it. He still cares for people—and companionship, thank God. But no, he's never taken any liberties with me, Graeme; I think he's well past that sort of thing. Of course we argue a lot, but that's what keeps us going. It keeps our courage up, keeps us together, makes our miserable lives seem almost real. Can you understand that?'

I said that I could. It made sense. 'Then he's all right with you? Apart from the squabbles?'

'If Jamie hadn't found me I don't know what I would have done.' She gave a wan smile. 'I suppose I can put up with that damned recorder for a little while longer...'

I felt a sudden urge to wade into the pool. I asked her if she had ever tried.

'Yesterday. First thing I did when I found it.'

'And?' I was apprehensive.

'Why not see for yourself?'

I rolled up my jeans past my knees and stepped cautiously into the pool. The familiar scrunch of sand and pebbles underfoot was exhilarating—even the slimy feeling of the small rocks and molluscs was pleasant, not at all like the interface. I waded slowly toward the abrupt line of demarcation that separated one half of the pool from its hazy counterpart 'outside.'

The water came up to my calves; my skin tingled. I stopped just short of the barrier. I stared down into the water. My progress had stirred up the sand and a myriad darting, flashing creatures. A solitary crab scuttled from underneath an overturned rock. I took a deep breath and waded forward—

—and left the 'real' pool behind me. Before me stretched the interminably grey and silent sea, the waves rolling in slowly toward the beach. The sensation of having my feet surrounded by water and firmly grounded in sand disappeared; the familiar surface of the interface was all I could feel.

I panicked and swung around. But Marion was still there, standing by the rock pool and waving encouragement; the bright orange towel blazed beside her like a beacon. I breathed a sigh of relief. For a moment I had been afraid I had lost her, that the greyworld had swallowed her up. And I could not bear the thought of losing her. Not yet . . .

She looked very serious and very, very vulnerable. She must have unconsciously allowed her tough mask to slip for a moment, and I felt that I saw her as she sometimes saw herself, but with one important difference. I thought she looked beautiful. I felt a hard knot form in my chest, and I briefly forgot the mystery that bound us together, and found myself wishing that this had been another time and another place and that we were part of the 'outside' world and not imprisoned in this ugly grey Limbo.

The magical moment passed away. Slowly my mind returned to its present problems. I trod the interface warily until I had moved through the intangible barrier and once again felt sand underfoot and salt water swirling around my bare legs. I breathed easier. And yet I could have cried for the experience I had lost.

Marion said, 'I could have warned you.'

'About what?' I muttered as I crawled back over the rocks and dried my legs with the towel.

'About what it's like, out there.'

I left the sand clinging to my feet until it dried. 'It is pretty scary,' I admitted. I folded the towel and carefully placed it on one of the larger rocks. Then I sat down beside her on a patch of warm sand. We didn't speak for a while. I was getting used to these long breaks in our conversation. I did not mind; it was all part of living in Limbo, like Jamie's melancholy recorder playing. Even without words there was harmony and balance in our relationship, and I was grateful.

I'm not sure how long we remained there, staring out over the silent sea. Time had ceased to dominate our lives. As Jamie had pointed out, it moved differently in the greyworld. It was as though we shared a time scale in common with our primeval ancestors. But eventually Marion stirred, stretched, and stood up. 'Come on,' she said, 'let's get on with our shoplifting . . .'

WE SPENT the next few hours wandering aimlessly through the shallow ravines of the greyworld that now represented the streets of Elwood and St Kilda and Balaclava. We passed the McDonald's restaurant I had visited only a few nights previously. This brought on a sudden rush of memories that I quickly cast aside. What was past was past. Marion was right: Only our future mattered.

Our efforts were rewarded with the meagre discovery of two handkerchiefs, a can of Coke, a toothbrush, and a packet of cheese biscuits.

'Not a bad haul,' Marion commented. 'If only we could find some water . . .'

I had been thinking about that. 'The rock pool,' I said. 'We could rig up some sort of a still. Boil some water in a pan or something. Place a bit of cloth—a handkerchief—over the pan, collect the moisture by squeezing it out into a container.'

'Sounds like a lot of work.'

'It is.'

'And it would take a long time.'

'But you would get water.'

'How much?'

I did a quick calculation, trying to remember what little bushcraft I had absorbed. 'Let's see. With constant boiling we could get maybe a litre of fresh water every three or four hours, depending on how—'

'That doesn't sound much.'

'You could make four, five cups of coffee. Well, it was just a suggestion,' I added lamely. But she looked thoughtful as we headed back to the house.

I fiddled with the miniature cassette recorder. 'It's funny how things keep coming through,' I said, more to myself than to Marion.

She said, 'I've often wondered what percentage of supposed shoplifting actually finishes up here.'

'So have I.'

We both laughed.

'I saw a car once,' she went on. 'The engine was still running. The keys were in the ignition and the driver's window was rolled down. But there was no one inside. I was tempted to get in and go for a joyride.'

'And did you?'

She shook her head. 'No, that was in the early times—before I met Jamie. I was too scared. I ran away. I went back, a few days later. The car was gone.'

'Gone?'

'Disappeared. Just like that.' She did not elaborate, but I could not help wondering about the fate of the vehicle. Had it been abandoned by some unlucky person who had found himself in the greyworld, or had it simply been 'displaced' while the owner went shopping in the 'outside' world? Perhaps it had slipped back in time? Confusion reigned again in my head. Would Limbo never make any kind of sense?

'I have a name for this place,' I said quietly. 'Do you?'

'I've never thought about it. It's just a grey world to me.'

'And me. But I also call it Limbo.'

'That sounds familiar. It's some sort of place for lost souls, isn't it?'

'Something like that.'

'As good a name as any for a prison,' she said curtly.

By now my bare feet—still encrusted with a little of the dry sand from the beach—were coping better with the interface, although I did not delude myself that I would ever match Marion's experienced walk. There remained a tension between my physical self and the invisible membrane that refused to disappear. It worried me.

Our dilapidated dwelling evolved slowly out of the greyworld. And I was brought to a standstill by a sudden memory.

'What is it, Graeme?'

I looked at the house and placed it in my memory. Back home, in the 'outside' world, it had not existed. Where it now stood I remembered only a vacant lot covered with all kinds of weeds and rubbish.

'Graeme?'

Marion tugged at my sleeve.

I shook my head, snapping myself out of an uneasy trance. 'Nothing . . . really,' I mumbled. 'It's just that, well, the house: There isn't one. I mean, for as long as I can remember there was only a vacant lot there.'

'You mean "outside"?'

I nodded. 'In Barkly Street.'

She shrugged. 'Well, then it must have come through a long time ago. Maybe nonorganic things remain here longer.'

It was an unsettling thought. Human beings needed sustenance to survive in the greyworld, but a building—how long could a building last?

When we arrived back Jamie was seated by the table, looking morose and unsettled. He lifted his head when we came in, but his expression didn't alter.

'And what's the matter with you?' Marion asked.

'It's gone,' he muttered.

'*What's* gone?'

'The bottle, lass. The beautiful Drambuie. Disappeared—just like that!' He snapped his fingers. 'It was sittin' right there, just a few minutes ago. Now it's gone.'

'Are you sure you didn't drink it?' she asked, in that slightly acidic tone she often used with him. Or was she trying to make light of the incident? Sometimes it was difficult to unravel her motives.

'Course I didn't!' the old man snapped. 'Wasn' time to. Meant to, though—but when I reached out for it it wasn' there! Only Drambuie that's ever come through. Blast. Makes it worse . . .'

Marion and I exchanged puzzled glances. 'We, uh, didn't see anyone hanging around outside,' I volunteered.

He shook his grizzled head. 'No, it's nothin' like that, lad. Somethin' else. Don' know what. I must have dozed off for a moment—no more, mind you. But sure enough the bottle's gone now, so no sense in cryin' over it.' He licked dry lips. 'Sure could have done with a sip, mind you.'

I stepped forward, depositing some of our haul on the crowded table. 'What do you think happened to it?' I asked.

'Dunno. Maybe someone back there remembered it.'

'Someone from "outside"?' I suggested.

I heard Marion draw in her breath sharply. For a moment the silence in the room was electrifying. Jamie gave me a curious look. I plunged awkwardly into the gap I had created. 'I was thinking about what you said— about us being forgotten by people "outside." Maybe someone forgot the bottle—and then remembered it. And if the bottle went back—'

'Now take it easy, Graeme,' he said. 'Who are we to say where the bottle went? Back? Maybe. But why not somewhere else? Moved on, so to speak.'

'Moved on?' Marion echoed. 'But where, Jamie? *Where could it have gone?*'

The old man shrugged. 'How the hell should I know? I only have theories, remember? Someplace . . . different. Different from here, I mean. Another stage, maybe. Where we are, why, it might only be some kind of—'

'Limbo,' she said quietly, a faraway look in her eyes. Her face had gone deathly pale.

'Limbo? Aye, that's a fair-enough description. Where did you come up with it?'

'Graeme.'

'Smart lad.' He winked at me. 'Well-read, too. Limbo, eh? As I recall . . . hm. No, we'll forget about that. Let's just assume that where we are now is a halfway place between the "outside" world and wherever we are destined to wind up. Now, it's no use either of you protestin'—I've been around this ghostly place longer than either of you and I've had plenty of time to think. And let me tell you, I've seen some things that scarce bear repeatin', lass—you take my word for it! And there's one thing I can tell you for sure: There's somethin' movin' around out there. Don' ask me what. But it's there. *I know.* A creepy, crawlin' somethin', movin' like a wind without a voice. Maybe when you've been around here as long as I have, you'll feel it too. I can feel it now.' He shivered, and looked away.

Marion kept her voice steady. 'Jamie, are you sure you're not trying to spook us? Things are bad enough already—'

'No, lass! Wouldn' think of it! You can trust me. I'm just tryin' to make some things clear to you which I think you should know. For your own good. Didn' mean to upset you. The thing is there all right, but with any luck it won' bother you for a long while yet—although to be truthful I wouldn' wish the experience on either of you. Honestly.'

Her face softened. She walked over and stroked his head. 'Oh, Jamie,' she said wistfully, 'I'll try and find you another bottle of Drambuie—I really will. You're right—I do sit around too much, doing nothing . . .'

'Ah, now wait a minute, lass. I never said—'

'No, but I see it now. I've used you—and after you saving me and all. You . . . you keep fighting.'

He gave her a despairing look. 'But what else *can* we do, Marion?'

She tried to draw him out of his melancholy mood. 'Well, Graeme's come up with an idea for distilling the seawater from that rock pool I told you about. All we need is some pans, some cloth—and a good supply of wood to make a fire on that strip of beach . . .'

He listened attentively, nodding from time to time. But the idea did not seem to arouse much enthusiasm in him. He echoed Marion's observation that it would take a lot of time and patience to reclaim even a small amount of water, to which Marion replied with a display of enthusiasm that surprised me, 'But I don't mind! We've got lots of time!'

'Aye, that we have.' Jamie looked thoughtful, but I felt his attention was only half with us; the rest of him seemed elsewhere—and troubled. While Marion continued to persuade him I let my gaze wander around the room, examining the scattered paperbacks and dog-eared magazines; then I started sorting out some of the foodstuffs from the refuse on the table.

Marion finally turned her attention to me. 'Come along, Graeme,' she said, 'and I'll show you the rest of the house. Jamie needs time by himself.'

She took my arm and we left the old man sitting moodily in his chair. He looked a little more cheerful than when we had arrived, but just as distant; he was obviously very disturbed by the disappearance of his valued bottle of Drambuie.

Marion led me down the long hallway. The next room on the right was bare save for a bundle of blankets on the floor and some old magazines. Another blanket had been drawn across the cracked window—for privacy? 'I sleep here,' she said. 'That's Jamie's room opposite.' The door was locked. She didn't bother to open it. We moved on down the hall until we reached a staircase leading to the upper floor. 'Nothing up there,' she said quickly. 'No reason to use it . . .'

She pushed aside a door and we stepped into what had once been an extraordinarily large kitchen. An enormous wooden table sat in the middle of the room and the cupboards were derelict with age. 'Can't use any of it,' she explained. 'Nothing works. No gas, water, or electricity. Isn't that a laugh? We do have some candles, some of those fancy decorative kinds—but we use them sparingly. I found a whole box of them once. The nights get awfully dark here . . .' I also learned that they had an oil lantern, of the type used for camping, which they kept in reserve because it had only a small supply of kerosene.

Marion opened the back door. Outside I saw a cracked path, choked with weeds, and beyond that a wild, tangled garden. It looked like a carnivorous jungle, something out of a horror movie. Roses and rhododendrons wrestled with creeping moss and ivy and fought a hopeless battle with the overwhelming grass. Flowers were withering for want of fresh air and sunshine—and rain. The odour overwhelmed me; the foliage was so intense, and the stench of decay so close, that I grew dizzy. Yet I inhaled the air greedily, regardless of the consequences. It was real. It was . . . tangible.

The rear of this remarkable garden gradually disappeared into the greyworld. My feeling of wild exhilaration soon passed.

'What do you make of the vanishing bottle?' Marion asked quietly. We stood close together, like conspirators, and I suppose in a way we were—in league against whatever unknown force had thrown us together.

'I . . . I'm not sure. But it kind of puts you on edge, doesn't it? Like that car you told me about, with the motor still running. It wasn't there when you went back, remember?'

She would not take the matter any further, but seemed determined to draw me out of the thrall imposed by the garden. 'Are you hungry?' she asked. 'I'm starving. Let's get something to eat—before it all disappears.' If she meant this to be lighthearted, then she failed. The mysterious grey fog clouded not only the visible world, but also my thoughts—and it seemed to grow deeper the more I thought about it. We were a solemn pair who walked back inside.

Jamie was still morose. He hadn't moved from his chair. He ignored us, lost in a reverie. I had never seen him look so doleful; gloom hung round him like a shroud. I wondered if after so long the hopelessness of our situation had got the better of him.

Marion prodded around among the pile of foodstuffs. She handed me a bread roll coated with sesame seeds. 'There's some margarine somewhere,' she muttered. 'Yes—there it is.'

I reached for the container and used Jamie's Swiss Army knife to slice the roll.

'There's a bit of sausage left,' she added, 'and half a bottle of lemonade—and the Coke we brought in.'

Gradually we put together a meal. Then we sat down, cross-legged by the still-smouldering fire, and ate in silence. A few small sticks of wood were all that remained by the fireplace; I did not think they would last very long. I knew that the fire was important to Marion; it was a kind of symbol. Keeping the small blaze alight was like keeping a beacon burning and helping to keep her dwindling hopes alive.

She looked across at the old man lost in his private thoughts. 'Jamie, we're almost out of wood. Do you feel up to finding some? You're very good at that sort of thing . . .'

He shifted uneasily in his chair. He looked for a moment like someone waking from a deep trance. He regarded us curiously, as though we were strangers. Then he blinked and muttered something under his breath.

'Jamie?' she repeated.

'Oh, all right,' he grumbled. 'I'll see what I can do. Mind you, I'm not promisin' anythin' . . .'

'We understand. But it *would* be sad to lose the fire, don't you think? It's such a comfort.'

He muttered again. A moment later he shuffled out of the room.

'Thank you, Jamie,' she called after him, but if he heard her then he made no answer. A short time later we heard the languid notes of 'Greensleeves' in the distance.

Marion sighed. 'I do so hope that song gives him some consolation. He's such a lonely old man, and he looks very sad and depressed at the moment.'

'It's hard to imagine him as a university teacher.'

'Oh, that must have been a long time ago. He's let a lot of things slip, but his mind seems sharp enough.'

I said, 'You're not arguing so much anymore.'

'Oh, that's nothing. Just stress. We had only each other . . . until you came along. Now it's different.'

'I hope he finds some wood,' I said. For the first time since I had entered the greyworld I felt an external cold —yet I knew that outside the house the pervading air of Limbo would be mild and pleasant.

'I'll see about setting up that still tomorrow,' I went on. Marion shared the last of her Coke.

'It's worth a try,' she said. 'At least it will give us something to do.'

I wondered if it was my imagination, but it seemed to have grown darker outside while we sat and talked. I studied the window nervously.

'Something the matter?' Marion asked.

'I'm not sure. But don't you think it's got dark awfully sudden?' My wristwatch indicated it was only three minutes past four.

We both stood up together. I had transmitted my own uncertainty to Marion. Her eyes were wide and a little frightened. 'He keeps muttering about a "darkness,"' she said uneasily. 'A darkness that comes and goes. He won't elaborate. I'm not even sure what he means. Let's go outside and have a look . . .'

She grasped my hand. Hers was trembling. I gave what I hoped was a reassuring squeeze and we went outside.

The greyworld had indeed darkened considerably. It was now impossible to distinguish one hazy smudge of a building from another in the 'outside' world. I looked up. Great rolling clouds were bunching together. Here and there I saw pale flashes that indicated lightning. I relaxed.

'Nothing to worry about,' I said. 'Only a storm building up "outside." And a big one, by the look of those clouds. See?'

But still she held fast to my hand, as though it were an anchor. She studied the turbulent sky with frightened eyes. I saw flashes of lightning mirrored in their dark-green depths and thought that even in her fear she looked beautiful. I wanted to reach out and hold her to reassure her, but something held me back; perhaps the time was not yet right and I did not wish to alarm her. And then from somewhere far away I heard the plaintive sound of Jamie's recorder.

'Only a storm,' I said softly. 'A summer storm. Remember them?'

The lightning continued to flicker and dance across the darkened sky, but no ominous roll of thunder accompanied it; that added attraction was denied us in our enforced silence. The pallid glow of streetlamps came on and the headlights of passing cars cut a dim swathe through the darkness. I guess that a sudden squall must be racing in from the sea, to judge by the thunderheads piling up and the scurrying shadows of pedestrians hurrying through the greyworld.

Seconds later the silent storm broke. The rain came down with what I judged to be terrific force, lashing the 'outside' world and all but obliterating the streetlamps and the lights of passing cars. We watched this terrifying display of nature's force from our cocoon of silence. The effect was uncanny and drove home as never before the extraordinary strength of the invisible interface that separated us from the 'outside' world. Not even a portion of the raging storm was audible to our ears . . . nor did a single drop of rain fall upon our upturned faces.

Water, I thought. *Nor any drop to drink . . .*

Without realising that I spoke aloud I cursed the interface and whoever or whatever was responsible for our bizarre existence. Marion hushed my anger and drew closer to me. Together we watched the storm rage furiously 'outside.' The abyssal darkness was eerie, but we gained confidence from the knowledge that it would soon pass. It was by far the most remarkable phenomenon I had witnessed since my displacement, and while I would have liked to discuss the implications with Marion, I could not bring myself to speak. She was so obviously emotionally involved with the storm and its effect upon our wretched isolation; I had no wish to disturb her. So I held her hand . . . and waited.

'Graeme . . .'

Her fingers fastened more securely around mine and she leaned her golden head upon my shoulder, as though the weight of isolation had suddenly become too much to bear.

'Let's go back inside,' she said softly. 'I . . . I don't like it out here.'

I agreed this was a sound idea. We left the front door

open for Jamie; I expected him to return soon. We only disengaged our hands when we were back in the front room.

Marion sat down on the faded carpet and stared glumly into what was left of the fire. She picked up some small bits of wood and laid them gently on the smouldering ashes. She shivered. Her face had grown hard again; I felt a pang of loss.

'I'm cold,' she said.

I realised how much colder it had become inside the house in the last few minutes. 'I'll get you a blanket,' I said, and draped the beach towel carefully around her shoulders. She rewarded me with a soft smile.

'Thank you, Graeme.'

I looked at the fire. 'Not much warmth,' I commented.

'It's a comfort. Jamie will bring back some wood. He always does.'

'It's warmer outside,' I reminded her. 'For some reason the temperature is always the same—'

'I know. But I hate the greyness. It . . . it gets *into* me.' She shivered again, and drew the bright-orange towel tight around her shoulders. 'You can go outside if you like. I'd rather stay here, no matter how cold it gets. At least I have real things around me. It's worth putting up with the cold to have them nearby.' She looked up. 'I'll light some candles when it gets really dark.' Her voice sounded . . . empty; drained of colour.

I leaned forward. 'Have you ever wondered if there are any others stranded here?' I asked, in an effort to draw her away from herself. 'Remember how vast the world was? Well, surely there must be many more people lost in Limbo besides us. If only we could find some of them! But the greyworld swallows everything . . .'

Marion did not respond, but my mind took off. I considered putting up some signs here and there, announcing our presence and location, for the benefit of any stranded strangers. I said as much to Marion, and this at least snapped her out of her mood.

'You mean, some sort of survival group? Band together and all that?'

I nodded.

She looked at me incredulously. 'Forget it! We've got enough to worry about just looking after ourselves on a day-to-day basis. Imagine the complications a larger group would bring! Not enough food to go around, arguments, fights.' She shuddered. 'No, if that's what you want you can count me out. Move somewhere else, find a place of your own. *But leave me alone.*'

I fell back in the face of her defiance. When I thought about it I could see she was right, and conceded as much. 'But you do think there could be others?'

She shrugged. 'Probably. But they'll have to look after themselves. In Limbo—your word, remember?—there can't be added safety in numbers, only more trouble. I think we three can manage to survive, but add even one more to the group and we would really be in trouble . . .'

I could see her point. The possibility that there might be others like ourselves—lost and lonely and in need of help—depressed me. But I knew Marion was right; our own survival came first.

'It's like living in a jungle,' I said bitterly.

'So you've finally noticed the analogy?'

'We spend nearly all our time foraging for food like wild animals.'

'I warned you about that.'

'A great, grey jungle stretching out to infinity.'

'And a prison. Don't forget that.'

Her sharp words brought me back to my senses. She gave me a knowing smile. 'Graeme, if you do feel like moving on . . . ?'

I hastened to reassure her this was not my desire.

JAMIE WAS gone for a long time. I wandered outside occasionally and peered into the darkness, searching for some sign of his returning figure. I hoped he hadn't got lost when the sudden darkness descended. The worst of the storm had passed over in the 'outside' world, leaving behind a deep cloud layer. This had the effect of making our surroundings gloomier than ever.

Marion passed the time reading a paperback novel. I admired her patience and resourcefulness but could not emulate her example. I prowled around the house like a caged animal. The analogy of the jungle was very strong.

Six o' clock passed by without any sign of the old man. I sat down beside Marion—who still had her head buried in a book—and said, 'What are we going to *do*?'

She didn't even look up. 'Nothing,' she replied, in a surprisingly steady voice. 'He's been gone longer than this before. We will wait. And endure. There *is* nothing else.'

Before I could reproach her I heard footsteps in the hallway. We both looked up as the old man entered the room. He looked crestfallen. Save for his recorder his hands were empty. His expression was pitiful when he said, 'I'm sorry, lass, but I couldn't find any. That storm kinda ruined everythin'. So bloody dark. Couldn' see anythin', not a scrap . . .'

Marion just stared at him. And then very slowly she got up and went over to him. She hesitated, then brushed his left shoulder. 'Jamie,' she said, '*your coat is wet.*'

'Eh?' He inclined his head to one side so that he

could see the patch of moisture on his coat. 'Well, I suppose a bit of rain must get through every now and again, like everythin' else. Especially after a storm like that. Nothin' remarkable about that.'

I said, ' "There are holes in the sky where the rain gets in, but they're ever so small—that's why rain is thin." '

They both gave me a curious look.

'Sorry,' I said. 'Just a few lines from a nonsense poem I remembered. Milligan, I think: Spike.'

Marion looked down. 'Jamie,' she said, her voice shaking now, *your shoes are wet.*'

And so they were.

'Musta stepped through a puddle,' he said.

'A *puddle*?' Marion echoed, incredulous. 'You mean there's actually water out there?'

The old man looked suddenly weary. 'Guess there is. But you'd be hard put to find it now.'

'Graeme'—she swung toward me—'we will have to go looking first thing in the morning!'

'Sure,' I said. But I felt uneasy.

'Christ, but it's cold in here,' Jamie muttered, and drew close to the tiny fire. Marion stood there unmoving, her gaze following him, her eyes wide and her hand still poised where his shoulder had been, as though her fingertips still tingled with the faint trace of moisture.

Jamie sat down, huddled forward. 'Damn storm. Couldn' see anythin' for a while. Lost me bearin's. Scared I was, for a moment. Cars swishin' silently by with their lights lit up and great sheets of lightnin' flashin' across the sky. No thunder, though. But that figures. Aye, it was a big one all right. But it's passed over now . . .'

'We haven't much food left,' Marion reminded him. Her voice sounded very distant.

'That I know. But what we have will have to do us until tomorrow.'

'Graeme and I have already eaten.'

'Then that's fine. I don't feel up to much, thanks just the same. In the mornin' we can all go lookin' . . .' He brushed his calloused hands across his eyes. 'Darkness,' he mumbled. 'Damned darkness.'

'It's only because of the storm,' I explained. 'There's deep cloud cover in the "outside" world.'

Marion said, 'I'll light some candles . . .'

Jamie gave me a strange look, then turned away. 'This is another kind of darkness, lad. It comes to me like a swirlin' mist, like cobwebs before my eyes. Damned nuisance! Just comes and goes.' He would not expand upon the curious nature of this 'darkness.' 'Go careful with the candles,' he called after the girl.

She paused in the doorway. 'We could use the lantern. It would give off warmth.'

'No. Leave that till we've nothin' else.'

She did as he advised. While she was out of the room I tried to get the old man to tell me something more about this special 'darkness.'

'Ah, it's like I said, it just comes and goes. Sometimes it's like a dark fog rollin' in. Nothing like it.' He rubbed his weary, watery eyes. 'If only it would leave me alone . . .'

He fumbled in the pockets of his overcoat and placed a can of baked beans on the floor near the fire. 'That's all I could find,' he grumbled. 'Beans. Can you imagine that? *Beans*. And not a scrap of wood. Poor Marion . . .'

She came back into the room, carrying in each hand a lighted candle set in a plate. She placed one on the table and the other on the mantelpiece. The feeble glow helped. 'Don't worry about the wood, Jamie,' she said. 'We'll find some tomorrow.'

'Of course we will.' But some of the spirit seemed to have left him. 'I . . . I think I'll be lyin' down for a while. Don't feel so good. Long walk. Fruitless. And the darkness . . .'

He got up and wandered off into his room.

I turned to Marion. 'Now what do you make of *that*?'

'He's been like this before. It's the darkness, isn't it? It always hits him this way.'

'But what is this special kind of darkness he keeps talking about?'

'Search me. Maybe he found it in a bottle. He's done that before, you know—and drunk it all before coming back so's not to get me going. Oh, let him sleep off whatever's bothering him. He'll feel better in the morning. He always does.'

'You've seen him like this before?'

'Not often. But enough.' She looked down at the can of beans. 'Hungry?'

I shook my head. 'Not really.' I picked up the tiny cassette recorder and began fiddling with it.

'Wish it was a radio,' she said wistfully. 'Then we could hear some music.'

'I don't think we'd pick up any broadcasts in here,' I said. 'Tomorrow I'll see if I can con Jamie into putting down a few tracks with that blasted recorder of his . . .'

That made her laugh. 'Or we could sing a few songs ourselves.'

I laughed along with her. It helped relieve the tension of the moment. Then she gave me a studied look. 'What are your plans for tonight. Sleeping out?' There was just a suggestion of mischief in the way she spoke. But I was in no mood to be so provoked.

'I'll stay here, if that's all right with you,' I answered.

'Course it is. Please yourself.' And with that she busied herself opening the can of beans with Jamie's fancy knife.

We shared this meagre supper. Later, when the cold night air inside the house began to crowd us, I helped her haul her makeshift bed into the front room. We reassembled the collection of old blankets and towels and clothes in front of the dwindling fire. It was still the warmest room in the house.

Jamie had not stirred, and on Marion's advice I decided to let him sleep. Perhaps some ghosts from the past had sprung up to haunt him in this godforsaken place.

Marion and I slept together, back to back for mutual warmth. We were suddenly too tired even to speak to each other. We managed a perfunctory exchange of goodnights and that was all.

Before I drifted off to sleep I heard the old man's recorder weaving its familiar melancholy tune. I was tempted to get up and go see if he needed anything. Marion must have sensed my urge because she mumbled drowsily, 'Let him be. He'll look after himself.'

So I settled back. We had extinguished the candles to conserve fuel. Only a pale glow radiated from the last embers of the fire. Soon total darkness would envelop us, but I no longer felt afraid with the girl beside me.

I found no consolation in the melancholy playing of 'Greensleeves.' I hoped the old man did. The sound of the recorder ended abruptly in midnote. I guessed Jamie had fallen asleep . . .

I WAS aroused the following morning by the urgent sound of Marion's voice and her hand shaking my shoulder.

'Graeme—wake up! It's Jamie—he's gone!'

I stared at her groggily, my mind heavy with sleep. She was wild-eyed and dishevelled. 'Gone?' I echoed.

'Where?' I was not sure what she meant; my fuzzy head could not take hold of her words.

'I don't know! I can't find him anywhere! Only this . . .' She held up the old man's recorder. 'I found it in his room. He wouldn't go anywhere without it. Oh, Graeme, what are we going to *do*?'

She slumped to her knees. She looked so miserable and frightened that I was jolted into full awareness of the situation. Jamie—gone?

I crawled out of the motley collection of rags that had been our bed. I ran my fingers through my rumpled hair, thinking, *We must look a pretty rough pair*. I could feel stubble sprouting on my cheeks. I considered—incongruously—growing a beard.

'Now hang on a minute,' I cautioned. I couldn't bear to see her so despondent. My body was still warm from her imprint and my heart went out to her. 'It might not be as bad as you think. He probably wandered off early, looking for firewood. He promised.'

'He said we would *all* go.'

'Yes, I know—but he might have wanted to give us a surprise.' The fire was dead in the grate. I added—almost in desperation—'I'm sure he won't be long. What time is it? See—only seven-thirty. Just calm down, will you?'

She said nothing. Just stared down at the recorder in her hands. And then: 'But he wouldn't have gone without this. I *know*.'

I could see it was no use arguing with her. 'Let's wait and see,' I said lamely.

'He kept talking about the darkness,' she went on. 'Remember? To him it was something . . . personal. Something he couldn't explain, or didn't *want* to explain.'

'I know.' I kept talking to comfort her. I had never seen her so distressed.

'I can't get over the feeling that something awful has happened to him, Graeme.'

I was not about to dispute her intuition; my own thoughts about the matter positively crawled with unhealthy possibilities. I was afraid of what would become of us, but I worked hard to keep up a bold front; no sense us both going to pieces just because old Jamie wasn't around . . .

Only then did I realise how dependent we had become upon him. An old man in ragged clothes playing the same old tune over and over again on his recorder . . .

We waited. And we waited. Time crawled around to ten-thirty. Neither of us ate. We couldn't. And still no sign of Jamie.

I said, 'He was gone a long time yesterday.'

'That was because of the storm. And he did take *this* with him.'

I sat down, picked up the cassette recorder, flicked it on. 'Let's talk.'

'About what?'

'Anything. To pass the time. No sense brooding. If he's gone, he's gone. We have to pull ourselves together.'

'I suppose so.' Marion was no fool, but her strength seemed to have left her and instead of the stern, sometimes scathing person I had known I saw now a lonely and very frightened young woman.

I could barely hear the whir of the tiny machine as it swung into action. I angled the built-in condenser mike to suit us both. 'You have any family?' I asked.

She hesitated for some reason, then shrugged. 'Parents. Three sisters, one brother—the eldest. I was the fifth in line. I'm not at all sure I was . . . you know, expected. I'm not saying that my parents resented me or anything like that. No, they were fair people. But I didn't have a very happy childhood. I know that's old hat, but I mean it. My parents were—are—conservative. And as I grew older, well, I wasn't exactly what you would call their favourite.'

Never having experienced sibling rivalry, I could appreciate only intellectually what for her must have been a very troublesome emotional time.

'What about you?' she countered. 'Did you have . . . anyone?'

'Only my parents.'

'No brothers, sisters?'

'I was an only child. It has its advantages, you know. For example, you're never in any doubt just *who* you are. Your personality doesn't get all twisted up with everyone else.'

That made us both laugh.

'I could show you the house I lived in,' I went on. 'But no—I don't think that would be a good idea.'

'Probably not. Too painful.'

She understood.

A long silence followed, broken only by the barely audible sound of the recorder. Then: 'Any special friends?' she asked suddenly.

I thought for a moment. A dark cloud settled over my past. Annette seemed so far away that she might never have existed. It was only here and now that mattered. And yet—

'Yes, there was one friend in particular.'

'A girl? Thought so—I can tell from your expression. What was her name?'

I told her.

'That's pretty.'

'So is Marion.'

She made a face. 'You think so?'

'Yes. It means . . . "the wished-for child." Same as

Mary.'

She gave me a curious look. 'I always thought it meant "bitter." '

'Well, it does in the old Hebrew meaning. But after the birth of Christ the name Mary and its variations took on a new significance.'

'Oh.' She smiled. ' "The wished-for child." That's a laugh!'

'Why do you take it that way?'

Her reply was guarded. 'I was never the success my parents hoped for. Robert became a biologist—he had a heck of a start! Josie, Allison, and Brenda all went into academic work. They're still "at school," so to speak. I . . . I dropped out. Couldn't face the rat race. You know how it is. At least you must have *heard* how it is. Well, Mum and Dad wanted me to follow in my big sisters' footsteps. But I opted out.'

'Why so soon?'

'I *hated* school. Everything about it. The rules, the regulations, the hours . . .'

It was a familiar story. I listened just the same.

'I couldn't study. Life was a bore and a drag . . .'

'So you left school and went out to work?'

'When I was fifteen. Boy, were my parents outraged! It seems ages ago now. Is it like that for you?' I nodded. 'Well, I worked mostly in shops. It's a grubby sort of existence, but it pays well enough, and you get to meet a lot of different people. Most of them are mean and ugly, though—the people I worked for, that is. Though come to think of it, some of the customers took a helluva lot of patience.'

'Not cut out for being a shop assistant, eh?'

'Hardly.'

'What kind of work did you like best?'

'The pet shops. The customers were nicer and I was

left mostly to myself. The bosses didn't interfere as much. Then there were the rock shops.'

'Rock shops.'

'Not music—minerals. Gemstones and all that scene. The bookshops were a bit of a drag; I never enjoyed lugging all that stuff around. And the bosses were neurotic. Say, are you putting all this down on tape?'

'Only for something to do. I can wipe it out if you want me to.'

'No, that's cool. I'd like to hear it played back afterward, see if I sound as bitter as I feel.'

'Maybe afterward we can sing a few songs.' That made her laugh. 'When Jamie comes back—' I didn't go on.

She shifted restlessly on the carpet. 'Remember how I told you I was visiting the city . . . when it happened?'

'Yes.'

'Well, that wasn't strictly true. Oh, I had come to see my parents all right. But you see, I had run away from them, oh, a year or so previously. Just had to, you understand? I couldn't take their pressuring me anymore. They wanted me to go back to school, get a degree. The usual garbage. And they didn't like my friends. That was pretty rough. Looking back, I don't think my pals were a particularly bad lot—but Mum and Dad dubbed them the "wrong sort." Make of that what you will. There was this one guy I liked a lot and—no, I won't go into that. But life with my friends was exciting and adventurous—it wasn't dull or boring. I was hooked. That is, until things got a little too adventurous and I wound up having to explain a few things to the cops.' She paused and took a deep breath. 'Oh, they went easy on me—first-timer and all that. I was rewarded with an enforced stay for six months at an agricultural college for first-time losers in the country run by—of all people!—the

Salvation Army. It fair drove me up the wall listening to their hymns all day. I broke out after a few weeks and headed back to the city. I had almost reached home when it happened...'

'Was it sudden?'

She nodded, remembering her own experience. 'So I wound up here, in Limbo, just like you. I never even got to see my parents. I've been stuck here ever since—with Jamie.'

I wanted to hold her in my arms and reassure her that everything would be all right, but I was gripped by an overwhelming shyness. I found that I could not bring myself to touch her, despite the strange intimacy we shared; there was something *spiky* about her emotional state that kept me at a respectful distance. I hoped this invisible barrier of thorns would not last forever.

The recorder whirred on. She regarded me thoughtfully. 'Your Annette,' she said. 'Was she... attractive?'

'Yes. Very.'

'A nice girl.' Derisively.

'More than that.'

'Sorry. I didn't mean to sound bitchy.' She stood up slowly. 'Come on, let's get the hell out of here. This place is giving me the creeps. I have to go somewhere.'

'To the beach?' I suggested, hoping that the rock pool would brighten me up.

'Why not? Perhaps Jamie will return while we're gone...'

But I don't think either of us believed that.

WE WALKED out into the greyworld. It seemed darker than before, although the sky was clear 'outside.' As usual, Marion led the way with her sleek, gliding movements across the interface. I followed her as best I could. I was becoming more adept with experience, but my walk was still clumsy compared to hers.

We ignored the sweeping, irregular grey masses of cars and pedestrians and headed straight for the beach. But when we arrived there we couldn't find the rock pool. It had vanished.

We walked up and down the great grey width of sand without locating it. Marion began to sob. Only then did I find I could put my arms around her and give her the comfort I knew she needed.

'It's gone!' she cried, her head resting against my chest and her small fists beating against my arms in frustration. 'Like Jamie. Like the bottle. *Gone*. We'll never find it. Never . . .'

I let her cry. It seemed she had been holding back an avalanche of grief and she needed time to disgorge it. She cried enough for the whole world—the world we had left behind. She certainly cried enough for me. And for Jamie. Poor fellow. Where was he now?

I stroked her long blond hair until she stopped crying and only dry shudders racked her body. Finally she sniffed and looked up, and I think that I saw her for the very first time. The barrier was gone.

She pulled herself away and brushed her hands across her face, a gesture reminiscent of tossing aside some stray strands of hair. A curious expression now took hold of her.

'What is it?' I asked.

She looked away. Her voice sounded very distant. 'It . . . it's the darkness. Like Jamie said. Wisps of darkness around the side of my head. They won't go away. Oh, Graeme!'

I looked quickly around. 'I can't see anything . . .'

She was crying again. She shivered and crept back into my arms. 'Can't you?' she whispered, barely breathing. 'Then . . . we won't worry about them, will we? But let's get away from here . . .'

We linked arms and made our way back to the park, moving for the first time *together*, with no hurrying ahead on her part. But defeat weighed heavily upon us. The greyness had become so concentrated that we could no longer distinguish one blurry object from another. We found our way back to the old house more by instinct than by design.

Jamie had not returned.

'Let's face it,' I said, 'the poor fellow's gone. Just like the pool.'

'But gone *where*, Graeme?'

'Up the line? Back to the real world? How the hell should I know? I'm sorry. I shouldn't have spoken like that. It scares me. I'll get us something to eat—'

'I'm not hungry,' she said.

'You've got to eat something.'

She sat down on the bean bag, arms folded. I scrounged around and found a bit of stale bread, some dried-out cheese, and half a can of flat lemonade.

I sat down beside her. 'Marion, I heard him playing his recorder last night.'

She gave me a vague look.

'You heard it, too,' I went on. 'But you were half asleep. I was just about to get up and go and see if he needed anything when you told me he would be all right, he'd look after himself . . .'

She sat up straight. 'Yes, I remember that.'

'Well, I lay there listening for quite a while, and you know what? He cut off in the middle of a note. Snap—just like that. I thought it sounded strange, but I was nearly asleep and I thought that he had probably dozed off. I wonder if I had gone in then—'

'Would you have found him?' She shivered. 'Probably not. He probably disappeared then.'

'We can't be sure.'

'No, but it seems likely. It wouldn't be like Jamie to fall asleep playing his recorder. He must have dropped it.'

The instrument lay on the table where she had left it, a sad reminder of the old man.

She leaned forward. 'Graeme, whatever are we going to do?'

'Carry on. Just like before. Only Jamie won't be with us . . .' What else could we do?

We managed to see the day out. I fooled around with the cassette recorder. We told each other stories and discussed our different lives—our youth, our escapades, our continuing adolescence. We talked about our first loves and broken hearts, vicious headmasters and understanding friends. About our hopes and fears for the future and the way the world was heading. We were very frank with each other. I think we kept talking because we couldn't bear the silence anymore. What we said didn't really matter when we stopped to consider our fate; I was convinced that we would soon be taken by whatever mysterious force had removed Jamie from our ken —just like the marvellous rock pool and the bottle of Drambuie. I watched Marion carefully, and from time to time caught her making the same brushing motion across her face.

We sang many songs—folk and pop—and even managed to share a few laughs. We had soon filled both sides of the first tape and I switched over to the spare— but not before we had played back some of the earlier stuff and been amused by our riotous singing and slightly hysterical laughter.

Eventually we ran down. When both tapes were filled I switched the machine off and stared at it for a long while. Silence filled the room.

'It's getting late,' Marion said. A sadness had crept into her voice. 'Are you hungry?'

This time it was my turn to say no. She mumbled something about 'having a good look for some food tomorrow.' She rummaged around the room for a long time with a determination that surprised me. Finally she emerged from a pile of paper cartons in one corner, holding aloft a bottle of white wine.

'I was hiding it from Jamie,' she explained, smiling. 'I had forgotten all about it . . .'

We drank a solemn toast to each other from paper cups. In another time, in another place, it could have been a magical moment, but I saw no lustre in her eyes and my only feeling was one of deep depression. My fears increased as the daylight waned.

When night closed down she lit the candles. She moved slowly now, like a sleepwalker, and I couldn't put it down to a few cups of wine. And there was a determination in her manner which had replaced her earlier uneasiness.

'Tonight we'll let them burn,' she said calmly. 'We can use fresh ones . . . tomorrow.'

'Of course.' I enjoyed the candlelight.

Suddenly she leaned forward, her hands hard up against the table. Her eyes were closed and all the colour had drained from her face. She looked as though she was about to faint.

'*Graeme?*'

I went straight to her. 'Yes?'

'Remember . . . what Jamie said . . . about the darkness?' She spoke with her eyes still closed, and with what seemed great effort.

'I remember.'

'Good. I . . . I want you to know that I . . . understand . . . what he meant. I can feel it too . . .'

'Like it was down at the beach?'

'Worse. Much worse. It . . . it's been hanging around me all day, but I didn't want to worry you.'

'But you should have told me!'

She shook her head. 'No,' she said firmly. 'One of us had to remain strong. And I needed you, Graeme. God, how I needed you!' A dry sob racked her slender body. 'It won't go away. I thought it would . . . but it hasn't. It seems to be closing in around me like a fist. Graeme, I'm afraid.' She turned to me in desperation, her eyes filled with tears. 'Hold me—*please* . . .'

She came into my arms and fluttered her hands against me like a frightened bird. She did not cry. Her grief was contained—and that made it all the worse. Her muffled voice went on. 'At first it was only trailing wisps of smoke, but it got worse as the day wore on . . .'

I could see only the familiar drab room, illuminated by candlelight. I said carefully, 'And what's it like now?'

Her answer shook me.

'Oh, Graeme—*I can hardly see you!*'

My silence must have frightened her. She grabbed hold of me fiercely and burrowed deeper into my chest. 'Hold me. *Hold me*. Please don't . . . let go.'

And hold her I did, through all the long and lonely night that followed, while visions of a ghost called Annette wandered in and out of my thoughts and I sometimes cried for all the dear things I had lost and the poor child in my arms.

We lay huddled together, facing each other under the pile of old rags we called a bed. Once, when I drifted off into a kind of half sleep, I was aware that she got up for a while. I could hear her stumbling around the darkened room (the candles had long since gone out), as though she were searching for something. 'What is it?' I mumbled. 'Marion, what are you doing?'

For an answer she slid back in beside me and placed a gentle hand upon my lips. 'Ssh,' she whispered. 'You get some sleep.' For a while she seemed to be fumbling with my jacket, then I felt her lips brush my cheek and heard her soft 'Good night' before she snuggled down against me. I waited, and after a while her breathing became strong and regular and my concern eased. She was going to be all right. We clasped each other as though we alone were life itself and nothing else mattered, and eventually I was so weary that I drifted off again into a fitful sleep...

I WOKE in the morning with empty arms.

The feeble glow of early morning filtered in through the curtains. *And I was alone.*

Without even calling out her name, without moving an inch from where I lay, I knew that she was gone and that I would never see her again. Like Jamie.

Beside me the 'bedclothes' were undisturbed. It was hard to believe that anyone had ever slept there.

Panic seized me. I struggled to my feet, casting aside the motley rags of our makeshift bed.

'Marion?' I called. *'Marion?'*

But there came no answer. Nor had I expected any.

'MARION!'

I ran through the house like a wild man, screaming her name until I was hoarse. The vast emptiness of the rooms mocked me and echoed my cry.

'MARION!'

I ran out of the house and careered blindly through the greyworld, slipping and sliding along the ominous interface, my previous skill forgotten. My world was now deep in gloom. I saw no shape or form to anything in the 'outside' world, just a jumble of meaningless objects. Eventually I ran out of breath and stumbled to a stop on the tingling interface. I squeezed my hands into impotent fists. There was nothing to strike out at—nothing!

For the first time I sensed an unfamiliar alien presence stirring all around me. I wondered if it was only a product of my confusion or if it was the same insidious force the old man had spoken of. His words came back to me: *'There's somethin' movin' around out there. A creepy, crawlin' somethin', movin' like a wind without a voice. I can feel it now . . .'*

And so could I. Skulking around the periphery of my thoughts.

'Marion . . .'

There was nothing I could do to bring her back. Now I could only wait and prepare myself for my fate.

For a long while I stood in a daze, wondering what to do. Then I turned my clumsy feet in the direction of the old house that had been such a strange home to me for a short while, and trudged back up the hill along the interface.

And when I reached the gate I felt the first faint wisps of darkness obscuring my vision . . .

FOR ME the end did not come quickly. I lost all track of time. I barricaded myself inside the front room and waited for the darkness to close in. Days might have passed—I had ceased to measure time. Sometimes I lapsed into delirium; occasionally I slept. But waiting, always waiting. I was too afraid to make any exploratory trips out into the greyworld in search of food. Instead, I scrounged like an animal among the litter in the room and found enough to nibble at.

Sleep was short—no more than a few minutes at a time. I would be jolted awake by the fear that the darkness had already invaded the room and would take me unawares. That was one thing I was determined would never happen. I would confront the mystery face to face —if darkness possessed any sort of face.

I muttered to myself and railed against my helplessness, waiting for the final moment when the darkness would engulf me and time and reason would stop.

The house was all I could cling to. It shored up my identity, but it could not give me courage—that had vanished when I had found myself alone.

Once I went out and opened the back door. The wild garden was gone, taken over by a steadily advancing blackness, blacker than any night I remembered, and it seemed to harbour within its depths the presence I had sensed outside.

I slammed the door and raced back to the front room, shutting that door also. It was then I remembered the cassette recorder . . .

I played back some bits of the tapes, but the sounds of Marion's laughter and her melancholy voice were too much to bear. I switched it off. Then . . . I wasn't sure what prompted my decision to put down on tape all that had happened to me, in as short a time as possible. I didn't expect that anyone would ever hear my words. It was only when I began talking into the little machine, and in the process erasing what Marion and I had put down, that I understood my reasons. The sound of my own voice is a gesture of defiance flung against the encroaching darkness. And while I talk, hurrying for fear that I will not have enough time to get down all that has happened, I see the greater darkness flow through the door like an ominous black cloud, bringing with it a mystery that matches the great wedge of ice that sits close against my heart.

'Hold me . . .'

Marion's words. Had she also felt this dreadful cold? But I am alone and there is no one to comfort me. Like Jamie, I will face the darkness alone.

In these last moments, before I am engulfed by the cold and the darkness and the presence, I see that Marion was right. I think we *are* someone's property. I think we *are* manipulated and pushed around by forces we are too puny to understand—like cattle. Or specimens on a slide. I find that I can no longer believe in such things as free will and personal motivation. We are all pawns in a game so vast we will never be able to confront the forces that control our destinies, any more than the tiny creatures in a rock pool can comprehend man or the tides that govern their lives.

But I have almost finished. The second tape has nearly run its course—and so have I. The darkness is so close I have only to reach out and touch it—but I won't. The thought makes me shiver.

I can no longer see the walls of the room; I am surrounded by an impenetrable darkness. When I last looked up—that was more than an hour ago when I changed the tapes—the darkness had only just begun to spread around the room. Now it has encompassed everything. Well, not quite. There is still . . . myself. But for how much longer?

Now I cannot see a thing!

The darkness has closed in more quickly than I was prepared for, taking my breath away. But it will take more in a moment; I must hurry . . .

I sense an eerie presence stirring within the darkness. It is certainly . . . alien.

There is a burning pain in my chest.

'Closing in around me like a fist . . .'

'MARION!' I hurl her name like a charm at the darkness, and the word is absorbed without an echo.

Dear Marion, where are you now? Will we meet again, if we are destined to be taken somewhere else by this awful darkness? Sweet child from another world, with your melancholy eyes and your blond hair and your graceful walk and a heart made bitter by too much living. And what of you, Jamie, old fellow? Have you found the Happy Isles, or have the dark gulfs washed you down?

Tennyson. Why should I think of Tennyson at a time like this?

Ah, I see your faces before me, pinned against the darkness. That much, at least, has not been denied me. I long to speak to you, to tell you how I feel, that at last I understand.

My lips move, but I cannot speak. No words tumble forth. I cannot move. The darkness has captured me. I feel a fist close tight around my heart.

If only I could

IT IS Monday evening, and I did not go to school today.

This morning I found a miniature tape recorder and a spare tape in a top pocket of my denim jacket. My first thought was that someone had planted them, meaning to play some kind of joke. I switched on the machine. Like similar units I have handled, the recorder has a tiny, tinny speaker—but I quickly recognised the sound of my own voice. And I was astounded. I cannot remember buying or borrowing the recorder, let alone recording anything like *this*.

I know there is a condition called temporary amnesia: could I, in fact, have invented and recorded this incredible piece of melodrama during some particularly inspired period, then have promptly forgotten about it?

But this explanation does not satisfy. I've never really been interested in drama. Novels and poetry, yes, but not theatre. Yet, if it's all me on these tapes, I am mimicking and projecting other people's voices, including my parents', with remarkable skill, capturing the most subtle nuances of speech.

Where and how could I have acquired such an ability? How did I get hold of such an expensive recorder? And what about the other small items crammed into my top pocket (I'll return to them presently)?

I am concerned about the implication of these tapes. It *is* only Monday, yet according to what I have heard on them I have been 'missing' for several days. It doesn't make sense. Maybe I'm on the verge of the sort of breakdown mentioned in the recordings.

A while ago I went downstairs and casually asked Mother if I had been, well, acting strangely over the weekend. She gave me a puzzled look, then smiled and asked me, Whatever did I mean? When I said, 'Well, you know, kind of . . . sick?' she just ruffled my hair affectionately and told me not to worry myself over nothing; that I had never looked better, although I could do with a good night's sleep.

I thanked her and came back up here. I ran through parts of the tapes again. Now that I have listened to them carefully, over and over, I am prepared to make what is called a leap of faith.

Suppose that everything in the tapes is true—that there really was a girl named Marion and an old man called Jamie; that somehow I lived with them for a while in a mysterious greyworld that apparently existed beyond the confines of normal space and time. A place I had called Limbo. Once I accept this—for the purposes of an exercise—I can then follow the situation, as documented, to a conclusion.

I consider the words as they have been recorded, and I am forced to confront some chilling possibilities. What if our conception of the world is restricted by our very humanity? Is it possible that the universe as we know it is only part of a single, colossal experiment, and that we can be manipulated by forces beyond our comprehension?

Is it not also possible that there are occasionally errors in programming this complex design, so that bits and pieces of it become displaced? Eventually there would be need for an accounting, with the displaced pieces being shuffled back to their correct positions. Relocation of inanimate objects and simple life forms would present no problems, but human beings would require special treatment. Because we carry a burden of time and memory, our environment would need to be adjusted accordingly, with space and time pulled around like toffee to restore the status quo.

Is it believable? I have every reason to believe it, although I cannot be sure how long my conviction will last or, more to the point, how long I will be allowed to hold it. The tapes may soon disappear as the necessary accounting becomes more precise, just as my memory of them might conceivably wink out and, perhaps, in time this book will disappear from your shelves and you will immediately forget what you have read.

Some discrepancies linger, but they are cancelled when I consider the evidence before me. For example, no matter how hard I listen to the tapes, I am unable to re-establish any satisfactory rapport with the greyworld called Limbo. I think of Marion constantly. In a way she seems more real to me than just a voice on a tape. *Why?*

I wonder how many Salvation Army farms for first-time losers are situated close to Melbourne. Not many, I guess. What if I did manage to find her, and she turned out to be just as I have described her on the tapes. Would she recognise me? I doubt it. Instead I think she would be inclined to regard me as crazy if I told her my story. Even if she agreed to listen to the tapes, I'm not sure she would be convinced.

And yet I long so much to see her, perhaps in the hope that the sight of her will trigger a revelation that explains all. But I'm convinced that the accounting I have conceived would not permit such a meeting. Oh, some small things might slip through from time to time (such as a cassette recorder and a spare tape), but nothing large enough or conscious enough to endanger the success of the great experiment.

Now there is only the present to concern me. Annette telephoned a few minutes ago. She sounded concerned and anxious to see me. We made a date for tomorrow night, because I couldn't say for sure if I would be at school again. By then I hope to have calmed down enough to face her. But for the moment...

I think once more of what was at the end of the second tape, immediately after the point where my voice breaks off in mid-sentence. There are exactly eighteen seconds of the strangest singing I have ever heard—half sad, half boisterous, one voice clearly mine and the other belonging to a stranger. Marion? I think so. The song is a rather bawdy version of 'Molly Malone', belted out with vigour and dissolving into hearty laughter. Just eighteen seconds, but as I remember it my scalp creeps.

I think I must have had time, before the darkness closed in and drew me back, to thrust the recorder and the spare tape into my jacket pocket. And I wonder if my fumbling fingers realised what else was in there—those other things I mentioned.

Two things. A crushed, faded rose. And a scrap of paper with a crudely drawn signature that says, simply, *Marion*, and two words:

Remember me.

Also in this series

IF IT WEREN'T FOR SEBASTIAN
Jean Ure

Maggie's decision to break the family tradition of studying science at university in favour of a course in shorthand-typing causes a major row. But the rift with her parents is nothing to the difficulties she meets when unpredictable Sebastian enters her life.

BROTHER IN THE LAND
Robert Swindells

Which is worse? To perish in a nuclear attack? Or to survive? Danny has no choice. He and his young brother, Ben, have come through the holocaust alive, only to discover that the world has gone sour – in more ways than one. And when the authorities finally arrive, help is the last thing they bring.

AN OPEN MIND
Susan Sallis

David had had enough of people being nice to him just because his parents were divorced. He'd got used to living with Mum and only seeing Dad on Saturdays. But then it dawns on him that his father might remarry and he was determined to do all he could to prevent this. Then Bruce, a spastic boy, appears on the scene and his life begins to look rather more complicated.

THE FIRST OF MIDNIGHT
Marjorie Darke

To eighteenth-century Bristol, where the slave trade continues to flourish in defiance of the law, comes Midnight, from the shores of Africa, bearing a sense of his own humanity which triumphs over the evil, scheming slave-masters. Befriended by Jess, herself a slave, Midnight battles for his freedom.

LET THE CIRCLE BE UNBROKEN
Mildred D. Taylor

The story of the Logan family's attempt to lead a decent life in racist Mississippi in the 1930s. A long, sophisticated book, but one which offers great rewards.

MARTINI-ON-THE-ROCKS
Susan Gregory

Eight short stories about teenage life in a multiracial urban setting. From battles with teachers to a young Hindu wedding, to the problems of being with the in-crowd: an extremely absorbing and contemporary collection.

THE PIGMAN'S LEGACY
Paul Zindel

Consumed with guilt and grief since the death of Mr Pignati, John and Lorraine determine to help another old man they find in his abandoned house. They force their way into his life, full of plans to make amends for their past mistakes, but things go very wrong and they begin to wonder if the Pigman's legacy is simply too much for them to handle.

CLOUDY/BRIGHT
John Rowe Townsend

Jenny often wondered whether Sam wanted her or just her camera. Ever since they met on Brighton beach he kept popping up in her life, suggesting trips to scenic spots to take photographs for a prestigious competition he had entered. Then Jenny began to suspect that there might be more to Sam than met the eye . . .

EMPTY WORLD
John Christopher

Neil Miller is alone after the death of his family in an accident. So when a virulent plague sweeps across the world, dealing death to all it touches, Neil has a double battle for survival: not just for the physical necessities of life, but with the subtle pressures of fear and loneliness.

TULKU
Peter Dickinson

Escape from massacre, journey through bandit lands, encounters with strange Tibetan powers – and beneath the adventures are layers of idea and insight. Winner of both the Carnegie and Whitbread Awards for 1979.

SURVIVAL
Russell Evans

High tension adventure of a Russian political prisoner on the run in the midst of an Arctic winter.

MISCHLING, SECOND DEGREE
Ilse Koehn

Ilse was a Mischling, a child of mixed race – a dangerous birthright in Nazi Germany. The perils of an outsider in the Hitler Youth and in girls' military camps make this a vivid and fascinating true story.

A LONG WAY TO GO
Marjorie Darke

The fighting rages in France, and posters all over London demand that young men should join up. But Luke has other feelings – feelings that are bound to bring great trouble on him and the family. Because nobody has much sympathy for a conscientious objector – perhaps the only answer is to go on the run.

THE ENNEAD
Jan Mark

A vivid and compelling story about Euterpe, the third planet in a system of nine known as the Ennead, where scheming and bribery are needed to survive.

THE GHOST ON THE HILL
John Gordon

An eerie story which shows the author's ability both to portray delicate relationships and also to evoke a chilling sense of the unknown.

THE TWELFTH DAY OF JULY
ACROSS THE BARRICADES
INTO EXILE
A PROPER PLACE
HOSTAGES TO FORTUNE
Joan Lingard

A series of novels about modern Belfast which highlight the problems of the troubles there, in the story of Protestant Sadie and Catholic Kevin, which even an 'escape' to England fails to solve.

KILL-A-LOUSE WEEK AND OTHER STORIES
Susan Gregory

The new head arrives at Davenport Secondary just at the beginning of the 'Kill-a-Louse' campaign. Soon the whole school is in uproar . . .

YATESY'S RAP
Jon Blake

It was Ol's idea to play the Christmas concert. His second idea was to get a band together. A most unlikely band it turned out to be. Half of them couldn't play, most of them didn't like each other, and none of them had ever been on a stage. And then Yatesy arrived, with his reputation for being kicked out of several schools for fighting.

BREAKING GLASS
Brian Morse

When the Red Army drops its germ bomb on Leicester, the affected zone is sealed off permanently – with Darren and his sister Sally inside it. Immune to the disease which kills Sally, Darren must face alone the incomprehensible hatred of two of the few survivors trapped with him. And the haunting question is: why did Dad betray them?